Tori Carrington

A FEW GOOD MEN

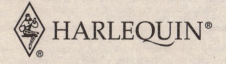

TORONTO • NEW YORK • LONDON
AMSTERDAM • PARIS • SYDNEY • HAMBURG
STOCKHOLM • ATHENS • TOKYO • MILAN • MADRID
PRAGUE • WARSAW • BUDAPEST • AUCKLAND

Recycling programs for this product may not exist in your area.

ISBN-13: 978-0-373-79449-2
ISBN-10: 0-373-79449-5

A FEW GOOD MEN

www.eHarlequin.com

Printed in U.S.A.

Twelve military heroes.
Twelve indomitable heroines.
One UNIFORMLY HOT! miniseries.

Don't miss Harlequin Blaze's first 12-book
continuity series, featuring irresistible soldiers
from all branches of the armed forces.

Watch for:

A FEW GOOD MEN by Tori Carrington
(Marines)
January 2009

ABLE-BODIED by Karen Foley
(Delta Force)
February 2009

ALWAYS READY by Joanne Rock
(The Coast Guard)
March 2009

THE RIGHT STUFF by Lori Wilde
(Medical Corps)
April 2009

AFTERBURN by Kira Sinclair
(Air Force)
May 2009

LETTERS FROM HOME by Rhonda Nelson
(Army Rangers)
June 2009

Uniformly Hot!
The Few. The Proud. The Sexy as Hell.

Blaze™

Dear Reader,

Strong, rough-around-the-edges heroes rank among our all-time personal favorites. So when our editor gave us the opportunity to create not one, but four true-blue USMC heroes for the first book in the UNIFORMLY HOT! miniseries, we jumped on board.

In _A Few Good Men,_ we focus on Lance Corporal Eric Armstrong, Lance Corporal Eddie Cash, Captain Brian Justice and Lieutenant Matt Guerrero, four hot combat-ready and combat-weary marines back home, either for good or on leave, struggling to adjust to life out of uniform (literally—when it comes to the four sexy heroines who steal their hearts). But if there's one thing they've proven, it's that marines don't give up easily. They'll keeping coming—and coming and coming— until the job is done.

We hope you enjoy every sizzling, sweaty, often grueling moment of Eric's, Eddie's, Brian's and Matt's journeys toward the happily-ever-afters they and all our men in uniform deserve. We'd love to hear what you think. Contact us at P.O. Box 12271, Toledo, OH 43612 (we'll respond with a signed bookplate, newsletter and bookmark), or visit us on the Web at www.toricarrington.net.

Here's wishing you love, romance and HOT reading.

Lori & Tony Karayianni
aka Tori Carrington

ABOUT THE AUTHOR

Multi-award-winning, bestselling husband-and-wife duo Lori and Tony Karayianni are the power behind the pen name Tori Carrington. Their more than thirty-five titles include numerous Harlequin Blaze miniseries, as well as the ongoing Sofie Metropolis comedic mystery series with another publisher. Visit www.toricarrington.net and www.sofiemetro.com for more information on the couple and their titles.

Books by Tori Carrington

HARLEQUIN BLAZE
113—JUST BETWEEN US...
129—FORBIDDEN
137—INDECENT
145—WICKED
212—POSSESSION
243—OBSESSION
249—SUBMISSION
335—TAKEN
359—DANGEROUS...
377—SHAMELESS
433—RECKLESS
439—RESTLESS

HARLEQUIN TEMPTATION
837—NEVER SAY NEVER AGAIN
876—PRIVATE INVESTIGATIONS
890—SKIN DEEP
924—RED-HOT & RECKLESS

Don't miss any of our special offers. Write to us at the following address for information on our newest releases.

Harlequin Reader Service
U.S.: 3010 Walden Ave., P.O. Box 1325, Buffalo, NY 14269
Canadian: P.O. Box 609, Fort Erie, Ont. L2A 5X3

We dedicate this book to Brenda Chin,
who never fails to inspire us with her vision
and eye for a great book.

And to the men and women of armed forces
everywhere, we offer our eternal thanks for your
dedication and sacrifices. OOH RAY!

Prologue

THE WHOOP-WHOOP OF THE CHOPPER'S blades forbade normal conversation so the five men were silent, each staring out the open doors at the Mediterranean island, but none of them seeing it as anything but the first stop in what would be a long journey stateside and home.

Matt Guerrero squinted against the sun rising in the east, a winter sun that held little warmth, shedding cool January light on the landscape and the situation that awaited him in Columbus, Ohio.

"Hey, Lieutenant, what say we jump out and swim the rest of the way?" Lance Corporal Eddie Cash shouted.

Matt grinned. "You start, I'll follow."

All five men chuckled and relaxed from the tense stance they'd taken upon embarkation from the _USS Stennis_ anchored a mile offshore.

Matt took each of them in. They looked too serious for men who were returning home from the front lines, either on break or for good. Usually the prospect of some fine sex and time off was enough to leave them all smiling like stupid fools.

Then again, this was no ordinary trip for any of them, was it? Not given what each of them faced at home.

Not given what had gone down a month and a half ago that had left one of them facing court-martial.

Matt tried to push aside the somber thought.

Eddie Cash was always the first to break the ice. A good kid who was quick with the wit and even quicker with his M-16. Although at twenty-five he wasn't much of a kid anymore.

Not that there really were any kids in the marines. Whether they were twenty or thirty-eight, like he was, the classification of *kid* was further away than even home.

Eddie Cash was returning to North Carolina to a woman he barely knew…and the kid—Eddie's kid—she would bear in a couple of months, a result of a shore leave romance that had ended when he'd shipped back out. Eddie believed with all the gusto of a tried-and-true marine that he loved her. She insisted she didn't love him and wasn't interested in marriage, but had been determined to have the child.

Matt pushed back his helmet. He supposed there were worse things. In fact, he knew there were.

He watched Lance Corporal Eric Armstrong slide his M-16 from his shoulder and hold it upright between his large, beefy hands. Hands that had seen more combat in the past fifteen months than Guerrero had seen in his entire first tour of duty almost twenty years ago. While he wouldn't admit it, he knew Eric was thinking about the woman he'd forged an online relationship with, only to have her disappear when he told her he would be on leave and wanted to see her.

Cybersex. Matt shook his head and looked at his own weapon, freshly oiled and ready to go. He supposed it wasn't much different from what he and his then new wife Ana had done years ago with racy handwritten letters to each other. But back then there had been no risk of their missives landing in the wrong e-mail box. And he certainly had known what she looked like and where to find her.

Thoughts of his wife erased the grin from Matt's face. She hadn't responded to the message he'd left on the answering machine when he'd called to say when he expected to be home. He wondered if she somehow hadn't gotten the message, if the line had gone dead while he was leaving it.

But he was afraid it was his entire marriage that was suffering a long, slow death.

He looked over at Lance Corporal Chris Conrad, the one man he'd met in his years of service that didn't deserve to be called a man much less a marine. He was responsible for the professional pall that hung over them like an impending desert storm. And if Matt had had his way, he wouldn't be on this transport with them.

Matt's hands tightened on his weapon and he ordered himself to stand down.

He forced his thoughts away from Conrad and shifted his attention to Captain Brian Justice. All Matt's personal concerns instantly paled in comparison to what he faced.

Justice was by far the toughest out of the group and their supervising officer. Matt recalled one of his lighter moments, when one morning Eddie had filled Justice's cereal bowl with shrapnel. Matt had nearly busted a gut laughing when Justice had actually spooned the metal into his mouth and commenced chewing.

But there was nothing funny about what Justice faced stateside. With a court-martial and dishonorable discharge hanging over his head, his eight-year career in the marines could very well be brought to a screeching halt.

Eddie came to take the seat next to Matt and elbowed

him, pointing through the open door. They were descending onto the landing strip.

Matt's gut constricted. In concern over what each of them faced professionally and personally. In fear that a wrong would never be made right. In dread for what waited for him at home. And with desire for a woman he would never stop wanting, but he was afraid no longer wanted him....

Eric

1

Eric Armstrong had come home on leave to surprise his online dream woman…instead, she was the one who'd surprised him.

He sat on his cot in the base barracks, staring at the name scribbled on a slip of paper he held in his hands. Much as he had in the days since he'd accepted the real name of "Samantha" from Tommy "The Tech" Onassis. After she'd pulled a cyber disappearing act about a month ago, he'd suspected Samantha had been an alias. But there was no way he could have known he was already familiar with the real woman.

"Are you sure this is it?" he'd asked the stocky Greek-American, whose finesse with a computer equaled that which most men put to use seducing a woman. Not that Tech seemed to have any trouble in that area. He used that overloaded, giga-pumped laptop of his to make sure he had women waiting for him—and whichever fellow marine won the lottery he held to go out on a double date—at each port of call.

Tech had stared at him. "You so didn't just ask me that."

And they'd left it at that.

Eric had walked around the base in a daze ever since, trying to decide what to do. If he were running on all cylinders, he'd walk away, go home to spend his leave in Texas, and forget all about "Samantha" and the deep impression she'd left on him.

But he was having trouble wrapping his brain around the truth.

His cell phone rang, earning him looks from a couple of his bunkmates. He picked up.

"Hey, where are you? We were expecting you home two days ago."

Eric stuffed the piece of paper into his pocket and smiled at the sound of his younger brother's voice.

"Hey, yourself, Trace."

"Are you going to answer my question, or just leave me hanging on the vine like an overripe tomato?"

Eric drew in a breath and exhaled. "I have some things I need to clean up here in Virginia first," he lied.

"The guys had a whole welcome-home barbecue planned. Killed the cow and everything. They're going to be awfully disappointed."

"I'm sure they'll enjoy the food without me," Eric said absently.

The line was quiet for a moment or two. Then his younger brother asked, "When do you think you will be home?"

Eric straightened, causing the cot to squeak. "Wish I could tell you, bro. Wish I could tell you."

"Is everything all right? You haven't gotten yourself into trouble or anything, have you?"

He thought of his fellow marine and supervising officer Brian Justice and the court-martial he was facing. Following quickly on the heels came the dark incident that had brought it about. A scene he feared was forever etched into the backs of his eyelids. "No, no. Nothing like that. Nothing I can't handle."

"Well, then, you make sure you give me a heads-up

when you know, ya hear? The guys will want to do something to commemorate your return." He chuckled. "Or at least be ready for it."

Eric grinned. It was nice to know he was missed.

He talked to his brother for a couple more minutes and then hung up, exchanging the phone for the slip of paper again.

He remembered when he'd first hooked up online with the mysterious woman named Samantha. He'd been in a chat room, just shooting the breeze, doing the cyber equivalent of flexing his muscles, and she'd popped up, calling him out on some of the false details he'd supplied.

"Me and the guys went into Bahrain last night and tied one on," he'd written.

"No, you didn't. You're anchored off the coast of Kuwait and there was no shore leave," Samantha had replied.

She'd been right. And he'd been smitten. A woman who withstood his bragging and not only managed to wittily defuse it, but stuck around to enjoy real conversations.

And then, six months in, their daily missives had ventured into sexier territory.

"What are you wearing?" he'd asked her, much as he had every other time within five seconds of logging on.

Her usual response was "a ratty old sweatshirt and jeans."

But not that day. That day she'd described, in sultry detail, the delicate lace of the new thong she'd just bought at Victoria's Secret. The red silk nightie that just brushed the top of her thighs. How her smooth legs and waxed delicates felt against her Egyptian cotton bed sheets.

Eric had instantly entered a period he described as being like a fully loaded M-16 with nothing to shoot at.

From then on, all he could seem to think of was Samantha. The fact that she'd never sent him a picture of herself, merely gave him general stats like five-six, one hundred and twenty pounds, combination of Denise Richards, Scarlett Johansson and Angelina Jolie, hadn't hindered his fantasies. If anything, not knowing what she looked like seemed to feed them. He'd lie in his cot at night thinking about the woman a half a world away, sleeping alone in her own bed. He'd go into a port of call with the guys and not really see the female sailors or locals hitting on him, his only goal to get to a cyber café where he could see if Samantha was available to chat.

He'd never considered that her name wasn't really Samantha at the time. He'd figured that since she'd refused to share her last name, the first had to be real.

He stared at the piece of paper in his hands and knew that wasn't the case. And that everything he'd believed in both his fantasy and real life had come crashing down around his ears.

"Samantha" was in truth Sara Harris…and Eric had been best friend to her late husband; a man who had saved Eric's life, giving up his own in the process.

"So I WAS THINKING that you and I could go to the symphony together," Sara's mother-in-law Gertrude Harris was saying. "You know how Howard hates the symphony and none of my friends… Well, they wouldn't enjoy the production as much as I know you will."

Sara took a bite of her chicken salad. She hated the symphony. Not that she'd ever tell her mother-in-law that. It would break Gertrude's heart to think that she'd been faking an interest all this time. Five years to be exact, when Sara had married Howard and Gertrude's only child, Andrew. She'd wanted so desperately to belong that she'd done a lot of nodding and smiling and not nearly enough speaking up.

"Just tell her, Sara," Andy had told her after the first time she'd sat through a production of Beethoven's First Symphony with his mother. "She'll understand."

"Yeah, she'll understand that I'm a liar and a fraud and the absolute worst daughter-in-law in the world."

Andy had chuckled and set about giving her a shoulder rub to make her feel better. And had progressed to rubbing other areas of her anatomy, making her feel much, much better.

But Andy wasn't here to make her feel better about anything anymore. And he hadn't been for a year and a half.

How young she'd been then, when she'd married Andy. Nineteen going on forty. And her top priorities were, first, to make her new husband happy. Second, to make her in-laws not only like her, but love her.

How much older she felt now. Much older than the five years that had passed.

"Sara?"

She looked up into Gertrude's face.

"Is everything all right?"

She forced herself to sit straighter and smiled. "Of course. What would make you ask?"

"I don't know…you seem a little distracted lately. Not like yourself."

If only she knew who she was anymore.

So much of her life lately seemed to be about going through the motions. After the two marines in full uniform had appeared at her front door to deliver the news that her husband had been killed in action, it had been hard enough to drag herself out of bed every morning, take a shower, and go to the small graphics design company where she worked. Simple things like eating became a chore, but she did it. Partly because she didn't know what else to do. Mostly because Gertrude and Howard had needed her to help see them through the sad ordeal.

Then came the day six months after the military funeral at Arlington when she woke up to discover that she hadn't allowed her heart to grieve the loss of the only man she'd ever loved. And her soul rebelled.

She'd spent a week shut off from the world, wishing she had been the one to go instead of Andy. After all, he'd had his family to live for. What did she have?

She'd had him. And now…

Sara looked at Gertrude. Now she had his family. And no matter how much she hated going to the symphony, or helping Gertrude organize Saturday luncheon and afternoons out with "The girls"… Well, putting herself out there, even as someone she feared she wasn't, it was all she had. And she would never, ever do anything to risk that.

Her cheeks felt hot. *Liar,* a little horned devil sitting on her right shoulder whispered.

She had done something to upset the status quo. The good thing was, no one but her knew that.

Well, no one but her and her late husband's best friend and fellow marine Eric Armstrong.

No. She was wrong on that account. She was the only one. Because there was no way Eric would ever know that her online identity of Samantha was really her. Would never know that she had been the one to reach out to him as an anonymous friend during that weeklong isolation, or that he had been her salvation, the sole reason for her to finally end her seclusion and continue an existence that sometimes loomed unbearable without Andy.

Then came the time six months ago when she'd given in to the feminine yearnings pulsing inside her, parts of her as neglected as her heart clamoring for attention. And she'd finally returned Eric's desire to take their online connection a little further. To venture into unknown territory with racy e-mails and instant messages. But rather than satisfy the sexual ache, their online flirtation had merely amplified it.

Until Eric told her he would be returning stateside for leave and needed to meet her….

Sara hadn't hesitated to erase Samantha's entire identity. The risk was too great for her to take. No matter how much it had hurt at the time to do so, no one could know what she'd done. Ever. She would never betray her husband's memory in that way. Never put his parents through the pain of knowing she'd indulged in provocative behavior with the man who had been her husband's best friend.

Never again allow herself to love a man whose job it was to put his life on the line for his country. She'd already lost one. Losing another would destroy her.

Gertrude was looking at her oddly again. Sara forced a smile. "I was thinking that I'd like for you and Howard to come over for dinner this Sunday," she said. "I could make that pot roast he likes so much."

"Andy's favorite." Gertrude immediately relaxed. "We'd like that. It's when we're at your house that… Well, that both of us feel the most like Andy might walk through the door any moment."

And therein lay the rub….

2

IT WAS ONE OF THOSE rare winter days when the sun slanted in just such a way that it was easy to be lured into believing it might be July instead of January. Temperatures were mild, the scent of the Atlantic Ocean permeated the air, and Sara's small house in Virginia Beach looked welcoming rather than foreboding.

She let herself into the one-story, two-bedroom bungalow she and Andy had bought five years ago and accepted the excited welcome and face wash she received from Truman, her four-year-old golden retriever.

"Oh, yes, you missed me, didn't you, boy? Yes, you did."

She let Tru out into the backyard to do his business, then put food out for him in the kitchen before going into her bedroom to change into sneakers and a sweatshirt so she might take Truman to the beach and enjoy the early sunset. It was only five o'clock and the rest of the dark night stretched in front of her like a black wall she couldn't figure out how to scale. As she slipped out of her low-heeled shoes and knee-highs, she reached out with her right hand to boot up her laptop, as was her normal routine. She took off her blouse and put on a T-shirt, then pulled the sweatshirt on over it, shaking out her shoulder-length brown hair before clicking to check for e-mail.

Her hand hovered over the mouse as she realized what she was doing. She was looking for a message from Eric.

How much she'd come to rely on those daily exchanges. It had been over a week since she'd been in contact with him. Worse, ten days since she'd deleted the e-mail account she'd used to communicate with him and, in essence, erased a part of herself.

She moved her hand from the mouse to the top of the screen and closed the laptop.

A moment later she had Truman on his leash, had filled a bottle of water, and left the house for the brisk, quarter of a mile walk to the beach, determined to forget that there would be no more e-mails from Eric waiting for her.

ERIC HAD HIS HAND on the door handle. He'd watched Sara pull her eight-year-old compact car into the driveway of the small house he'd visited on countless occasions, then go inside. It was the first time he'd seen her since before Andy's death. And the reality hit him full force, like the forceful butt of a weapon to the stomach.

He had the hots for his best friend's girl....

It was the first thought that went through his mind. A thought he'd never expected to have. Sure, Sara had always been attractive, but she'd always been Andy's girl. Off-limits. It had never even crossed his mind to think of the possibility of anything more. Partly because marines didn't go screwing around with other marines' women. (Well, good marines didn't, anyway.) Mostly because Andy and Sara had been so much in love that it had sometimes been awkward to be around them.

He hadn't gone to Andy's funeral. The Corps had offered to fly him back for the event, but he'd refused. He'd lost his best friend, but he still had friends in his unit that depended on him. And the enemy that had taken Andy's life was still a threat to the others. He couldn't leave them behind.

Eric closed his eyes and bounced the back of his head against the seat. Who was he shitting? He hadn't had the guts to face Sara or Andy's parents. Had been too big of a coward to admit that despite everything he'd done, he had been unable to save Andy.

And now here he sat, trying to reconcile that life then with life in the here and now. Remembering how happy the couple had been…and how hot he'd been for the woman named Samantha with whom he'd shared a closeness he'd never had with another human being outside the brotherhood of the marines.

He forced his thoughts outward.

Sara looked so much like the woman he remembered, yet not at all. He supposed the new filter he viewed her through was to credit. But there were physical changes, as well. For one, she'd cut her hair. Where the honey-brown strands had been almost waist-length before, now the ends barely touched her shoulders. And he could tell even under her loose clothing that she'd gotten thinner. Her once va-va-voom curves were now almost girlishly slight. She even seemed to hold herself differently, as if she no longer had the strength to hold herself upright, as if her shoulders bore the weight of the world and she was a straw away from collapsing altogether.

During his conversations with Samantha, he'd never really imagined what she'd looked like beyond the little tidbits she fed him, which could or could not have been the truth. He'd look at female marines and wonder, when any of them bore the same physical traits. Take in women who passed during shore leave and contemplate any possible similarities. So sitting there in his car now, he didn't experience disappointment. If anything, seeing her in person, despite the truth of her identity, merely made him want her more.

He started to pull the handle to get out of the car, unsure of what he might say or do when he came face-to-face with her, but sure that he had to do something.

Instead, he watched as Sara exited the house again, this time wearing sneakers and a USMC sweatshirt, patting a panting golden retriever before jogging down the block in the opposite direction.

Eric waited until she was out of sight and then scrubbed his hands against his face. What in the hell was he doing?

He didn't have clue. But whatever it was, he had to do it now. Fast. Before he was faced with another sleepless, endless night that was worse than anything he'd experienced except during a lull on the battlefield….

THE BEACH WAS ALMOST empty, a person here and there apparently out for the same reason Sara was, to enjoy the unseasonably warm evening and take in the sun setting in the west. She tossed a piece of driftwood and Truman took off after it, leaving her to stare out into the dark horizon of the Atlantic. Waves crashed against the shore, the roar drowning out most of her own thoughts and spraying the hem of her jeans with salt water. Truman brought the stick back and she bent to pet him, talking to the only male who had shared her bed in the past eighteen months.

"Good boy." She scratched him under the chin and then raised the wood above her head. He barked, ran a couple of feet, and then turned back and barked again, ready for the next round.

It was getting dark fast, the sun already having sunk below the fence of stout buildings lining the beach. The instant it did, the air seemed ten degrees cooler. She threw the wood and then pulled the sleeves of her sweat-shirt down to cover her hands and crossed her arms.

She'd long ago forced herself not to think about how many times she and Andy had walked this same stretch of beach, in the beginning alone and arm in arm as a couple, then later with Truman. She'd come to under-stand that if she stopped doing everything that they used to do together, then she would stay locked up in the house and do nothing at all.

She squinted into the growing dusk, trying to make out Truman in the distance. She hadn't thrown the stick that far, had she?

There. There he was. Standing by the dunes some hundred feet up, his tail wagging a million miles a minute. She moved closer, thinking he might have found a bird's nest or a crab or other small animal.

Then she saw him.

The man in fatigues who was crouched down petting the retriever.

Sara's heart hiccupped in her chest.

Andy...

How many times had she dreamed scenes like this? Of Andy popping back up into her life as if he'd never been gone? As if he'd never shipped out to serve first in Afghanistan and then later in Iraq? Too many to count. But none of them had ever been this vivid. This real.

The man spotted her and gave Truman a final pat before rising to his feet. The heart that had hiccupped now surged up into her throat, threatening to choke her. She wasn't losing her mind. There was a man there. A man in fatigues. But it wasn't Andy. On closer inspec-tion, he looked nothing like her late husband.

Where Andy had been short and stocky, this man

was tall and lean, although no less powerful. Where Andy had had blond hair, this man's close-cropped cut was dark. Where Andy had always been ready with a smile, this man had frown lines etched deep into his striking face.

Sara's footsteps slowed and then stopped altogether three feet from him, shimmering need pooling low in her stomach.

"Hi, Sara," Eric Armstrong said, the greeting nearly lost in the sound of the surf. "Or should I say Samantha?"

3

ERIC STOOD STOCK-STILL, staring into Sara's confused face, watching emotions slide like clouds across the setting sun. When she hadn't immediately returned to her house, he'd shadowed her footsteps, following her to the beach. There, he'd found her hugging her arms around her slender body, looking so small against the endless sea that he wanted to encircle her with his own arms.

Now, her lips popped open, as if needing to say something, but without the words to say it.

God, he'd never really realized how tantalizing her mouth was before. How downright naughty. Her lips were provocatively full, the upper larger than the lower. He couldn't seem to drag his gaze from them, wanting to trace the lines with his tongue.

The minute he'd come face-to-face with Sara, she'd stopped being merely "Samantha" or Andy's widow... she'd become a woman to whom he felt an irresistible attachment. With whom he'd joined virtual hands when he'd most desperately needed human touch.

The waves crashing against the beach mimicked the need surging within him.

"Eric..."

The wind snatched the softly said name from her even as he leaned forward to claim what it seemed he'd been waiting his entire life to have.

Her lips were moist and cool, the tang of seawater only adding to their appeal. Eric groaned and curved his hand around to the back of her neck, pulling her closer, demanding a deeper meeting. Sara complied, parting her lips to allow him to plunder the depths of her mouth with his tongue.

It was both the greatest pleasure he'd ever known and the greatest torture. He wanted to follow the desire in him to its natural conclusion, to fulfill all that he'd dreamed about over the past six months, the thoughts of which had kept him alive, and claim Sara body and soul right there on the beach. But he couldn't. Not because it was a public place and the act would be behavior unbecoming, but because while he tasted the sea on her lips, he became aware of the tang of salt from another source: her tears.

Eric groaned and broke contact, drawing her into his arms instead. She snaked her hands so that they grasped his shoulders from behind, her face tucked into his chest.

"God, oh, God, Eric…I'm so, so sorry. This…you and me…" She drew back.

He marveled at the dampness in her eyes glistening like the stars beginning to emerge on the eastern horizon. "I should never have contacted you. Should never have let things get out of hand…"

"Shh. We don't have to talk about that now." Eric found it impossible to swallow past the dryness of his throat. "I just want…need to hold you right now. Please. Just for a little while."

Her response was instant and complete. She burrowed further into his chest, her hip resting against his arousal. Eric closed his eyes and rested his chin on the top of her sweet-smelling head. In that one moment, he knew that if the option were offered him, he'd sell his soul to the devil in order to remain like this with Sara forever.

AN HOUR LATER BACK at her house, Sara felt as if she was violating some sort of unwritten code. Against her better judgment, she'd invited Eric in. He now sat in the old wood rocker next to the cold fireplace, holding a beer in his hands, the chair looking comically too small to hold his large frame.

She'd forgotten how big he was. Much larger than Andy had been. He seemed to fill every corner of the house with his presence. Something lost not even on the dog; the golden retriever lay at Eric's boots, his head on his paws while his watery eyes watched his every move in case there was another pat in the offing.

"I…I think the pasta must be done," Sara said quietly, breaking the silence that had settled between them.

She couldn't have ducked out of the room more quickly had there been a pack of coyotes nipping at her heels. It wasn't until she was alone in the kitchen again that she allowed herself a deep breath that did nothing to steady her.

What was he doing here?

She leaned a shoulder against the refrigerator, having imagined Eric's return countless times in her dreams. Her fantasies, really. Harmless musings that found him claiming her mouth the way he had on the beach and much, much more.

Of course, she'd never intended for them to come true. Had been convinced that she'd done a good job covering her cyber tracks.

How had Eric found out it was her? Was it something she'd said along the way? Oh, God, had he known all along?

"I think I have you figured out," Eric had written three months ago.

Sara's fingers had hovered over the keyboard, afraid to respond, wondering if she should shut down, pretend she hadn't heard what he'd said. She hadn't wanted it to be over. Needed for exchanges between her and Eric to continue for as long as she could safely arrange it.

"There's a bad girl lurking within you, Samantha. And I want to tempt her out."

She'd relaxed when he'd used her alias. He hadn't been talking about her real identity at all, but responding to her sometimes-raunchy posts about what she'd like to do to him if they were in the same room together.

"Sara?"

The sound of Eric's voice behind her nearly made her jump out of her skin.

The pasta!

She forced herself to take the pan from the burner and emptied the contents into a colander in the sink, following with a burst of cool water to cease the cooking process. No matter that her fingers burned from where she'd left the metal handle over the heat, her mind kept marrying the contents of their e-mails to each other with the fact that they now were in the same room.

And damn her wanton soul, she wanted to act out on every one of those cyber fantasies. Her favorite of which had taken place right here in this room.

"How can I help?" Eric asked.

His voice sounded right behind her, too close, too intimate.

The bottom dropped out of her stomach, making her feel oddly weightless. She turned to ask him to wait in the other room until she finished, to tell him that she couldn't think when he was this close…and found herself unable to say anything at all.

He stood with his hands jammed into the pockets of his fatigues as if trying to keep them from doing something else. The saying, "idle hands are the devil's playthings," rang through her mind…and immediately trailing it was, *I want to be that bad girl.*

She stepped the few inches necessary to bring her within touching distance, raking her gaze over his fine, male physique. Damn, but marines had to be the sexiest guys on earth. Raw, solid muscle and deadly intent. And if she was correct, Eric had just put her directly in his sights.

Sara leaned in to kiss him, possessed by a flash of desire to yank fantasy into mind-blowing reality. He didn't hesitate to return her kiss, his groan reaching inside to a place she'd long forgotten about. A place that had been hollow, empty, for much too long and now clamored for attention, demanded to be filled. Pure, unadulterated need zinged through her veins. She tugged his khaki shirt from his waist and he sucked in his stomach to help her. Finally, her fingers were touching the rippling waves of his muscles. Hot, so strong. Her mouth watered and she kissed him more deeply even as he hauled her sweatshirt up and off, barely breaking contact before she melted against him again, flesh against flesh.

She wanted to feel all of him…now.

She couldn't seem to take his belt off fast enough, and the same applied with him and her jeans. Finally, they each abandoned their efforts and focused on their own clothing until nothing separated them but unwanted air.

Sara knew a heartbeat of pause as she stared at the exquisite male specimen in front of her. Eric could easily have been carved from granite, standing at least six-three without a cell of unwanted weight on him anywhere. His prime physical condition made him virtually ageless even though she knew he was thirty.

He seemed to be asking with his gaze alone if she was sure she wanted to do this. That even now if she wanted to turn back, he would. The knowledge made her grateful…and all the more determined to have him….

SWEET JESUS, SHE WAS everything and more than he'd imagined.

Eric wrapped his arms around the hotly naked woman who stepped closer to him. She was soft and warm where he was cold and hard. And she smelled better than anyone had the right to. A bit of lavender with the tangy scent of the sea.

And her mouth…dear Lord, her mouth was the thing of which dreams were made.

He couldn't have been more surprised when Sara had stepped into his arms. He could have sworn she'd been about to throw him from the kitchen. Ever since they'd returned from the beach, she'd been antsy and uncomfortable in his presence.

Then she'd turned and kissed him and he'd forgotten about everything he'd wanted to say to her and focused on everything he'd been waiting to show her instead.

Every moment of every long night of the past six months were packed into his kiss. If he could devour her, he would. She tasted like salvation and pure temptation combined. Her tongue was merciless, dipping in and out of his mouth so that he felt like he was chasing it, chasing her. He raised his hands to rest on either side of her head and held her still, breaking contact briefly to stare deep into her eyes, and then leaning in for another taste. She clutched his wrists in her hands.

The two of them stood there, completely naked, just kissing for a time Eric was helpless to measure. He couldn't remember the last time he'd been with a woman, much less only kissed her when he could be doing much more.

She made a small sound at the back of her throat and he smiled, finally moving his hands from her head to her shoulders, and then down over the hot silk of her back. So long…so graceful. He pressed his fingers along the line of her spine, following it down to the high swell of her bottom. Then farther still, dipping into the shallow crevice inward until he probed her swollen womanhood from behind. He was surprised to find her so wet, so ready.

He groaned and picked her up. She automatically curved her legs around his hips, sandwiching his erection between her engorged labia. He turned her toward the kitchen island and sat her down, resisting the urge to enter her to the hilt right then and there. Instead, he reached for his discarded pants and took out the single condom there.

"I'm…I'm on the pill," she whispered into his ear before he sheathed himself.

He pulled back slightly to look at her.

"I…I never stopped taking it." She licked her lips, her pupils dilated so that her eyes were nearly black with need.

He kissed her deeply…and still sheathed himself. Confusion registered on her face.

"My dad always told me that you should always protect a lady," he said.

She opened her mouth to protest as he hauled her hips closer to him until she was on the edge of the counter and entered her.

Whatever words she might have uttered were eclipsed

by a soft gasp. Her eyelids fluttered closed and she arched her body, sensation appearing to take over. He helped her lie back against the counter. Eric's blood surged double time, her immediate response to their joining heightening his own reaction.

He'd waited so damn long for this. Too long. He planned to take his time getting to a destination that he had only dreamt about.

He grasped her hips and withdrew, wondering at the sight of his tanned, rough skin against her pale softness. She clasped his wrists and wriggled against him, hungry for what he'd only given her a taste of. He sank into her to the hilt again, gritting his teeth to keep from coming too soon.

She felt so good. Hot, wet, inviting.

"Please," she whispered, moving her head from side to side. "Please make love to me…"

And he did….

4

Sara rolled over in bed, pressing herself against the warm body next to her.

"Andy…"

It was a dream she'd had a thousand times before. Of waking up next to her husband…only to find he wasn't there. And she always cried.

But this was the first time someone actually comforted her.

"Shh." Arms encircled her.

Sara burrowed her nose against a rock-hard chest, clutching to the impenetrable wall that could protect her from everything. Her grief, her fears, the world.

Then she realized whose arms held her. And what name she'd said in her half sleep.

She rolled quickly away from Eric, the night before rushing back in snippets of sweaty flesh, soft cries and red-hot passion.

"I'm sorry," she said, reaching for her robe.

"Don't be. I miss him, too."

She looked over her shoulder at him. He looked so damn sexy lying against the pillows, the top sheet draped dangerously low across his hips.

"Yes, but I don't think you'll be calling anyone else by his name."

He glanced away, and she glimpsed the pain he must be feeling but was trying to hide.

"I'm going to be late for work," she said.

"It's Saturday."

"I work Saturdays."

Liar. Worse, she suspected he knew that. They'd talked about their hours during their many conversations and she'd complained about the nine-to-five grind and how she wished she could work from home with flex hours because sometimes she was best inspired during her time off.

Truman came in, toenails clicking against the wood floor, tail wagging, tongue lolling.

"I'll make breakfast and take Tru for a walk," Eric offered.

"I don't eat breakfast and I'll take care of Truman," she countered.

She gathered the clothes she needed and headed for the bathroom. Before closing the door, she turned to look at where he still lay, grinning at her as if he hadn't a care in the world.

Her heart skipped a beat.

Neither of them said anything for a long moment. Sara watched as the smile slid from his face.

He cleared his throat and propped himself up on his elbows, almost causing the sheet to drop lower. "Would you like me to leave?"

"Yes."

ERIC FELT LIKE HE'D taken a rifle butt to the gut.

Last night…well, last night had been one of the best nights he could remember experiencing in a long, long time. Merely holding Sara postsex and listening to her soft snores had made him feel more of a man than the past five years in the service.

Of course, her calling out Andy's name this morning he could have done without.

He ignored the pain that made it almost impossible to breathe, trying to conjure up a response.

Sara's brow wrinkled. "Did you just expect to stay here your entire leave?" she asked.

Yes, he realized, he had. They'd made such a connection that despite the considerable obstacles they faced, he'd assumed that once she let him into her house, she'd let him in all the way.

How wrong he'd been.

He scratched the back of his head and stripped the sheet off, moving to sit on the side of the bed. He noticed the way she watched his movements, especially a particular area of his anatomy with which she'd become quite intimately acquainted the night before, yet now apparently appeared embarrassed to see.

"I don't get it," he said under his breath. "You're like a faucet alternately running hot and then cold."

"Would you prefer lukewarm?"

"I prefer a consistent temperature."

"Sorry if I'm not made of metal with knobs you can adjust." She picked up his clothes with jerky movements and tossed them to the bed. His T-shirt hit the side of his head and stayed there so that he had to drag it off.

"What did you think when I disappeared from the Internet?" she asked, giving up her efforts and stopping to stare at him. "That I was playing hard to get? That if you showed up on my front step I'd throw open the door and welcome you into my bed?"

Her cheeks pinkened at her words. Eric didn't speak the obvious because both of them knew that in the end, that's exactly what she'd done.

"I don't need…" She gestured with her hand. "Want

any of this, Eric. I'm not up for a relationship with any-one, much less my late husband's best friend."

"So you'd rather continue to play the role of grieving widow?"

"What?" she whispered. What color had seeped into her cheeks drained out.

Eric sighed and ran his hand over his close-cropped hair. "That didn't come out the way I meant it to."

"Well, what way would you have preferred it to come out? Because from where I stand, there aren't very many ways to mean what you just said."

"Then let me take it back."

She shook her head slowly back and forth. "You should know that you can't put the bullets back in the gun after they've been shot."

"Damn it, Sara." Eric stood up and faced her.

She turned away. "Please…just go."

She disappeared into the bathroom and he was left with little alternative as the door clicked closed behind her.

Truman's soft whine brought his gaze down to the questioning canine.

"You think you're confused?" he asked the mutt.

He got dressed, gathered his things and headed for the front door, Truman following his every move.

SARA CLEARED the dinner plates from the dining-room table and brought in the apple pie she'd made from scratch. Her father-in-law had moved his chair back to make more room for his expanding stomach and rubbed the area in question, a satisfied smile on his face, while her mother-in-law stood in front of the banquet against the wall, picking up the photos there as she did every time she visited. Nearly every shot contained Andy. On the first vacation together in Colorado, their first anniversary,

Christmas with the in-laws…every photo marked a moment in their lives that would never be repeated.

"We had a surprise visitor yesterday," Gertrude said, putting down a shot of Andy and Truman as a puppy.

"Oh?" Sara used the server to cut the pie and picked up a dessert plate.

"Eric Armstrong dropped in as if he'd parachuted from a C-150."

"C-130," Howard corrected.

Neither of them seemed to notice that Sara had dropped half a piece of pie onto the white tablecloth.

Gertrude turned from the banquet. "You remember Eric, don't you?"

"Sure, I remember him." If they only knew that she had memories to draw on that were much more recent than their own.

Howard picked up his fresh fork to dig into the pie. "He said he stopped by here to pay his respects."

Gertrude looked at him. "You didn't tell me that."

He shrugged. "Didn't think I had to. He was Andy's best friend. He was there when he went down. Of course he'd want to see his widow."

"Yes, but why didn't you tell me?"

Sara was glad the two were too occupied with each other to see her reaction to the news that Eric had told them he'd stopped by there.

She tried to stop her hands from shaking as she handed Gertrude her pie.

"You're not going to have any?" she asked.

"No, no, I'm…" She swallowed hard. "I must have eaten too much pot roast."

"You didn't eat any at all. Howard ate enough for all three of us."

He chuckled, his mouth full of pie.

"You're getting too thin, Sara. Is everything okay? You barely eat when we go out, your clothes are at least one size too big, if not two."

Howard looked at her. "She looks all right to me."

Gertrude gave an eye roll. "Of course, you would say that. Men don't notice anything until it's waving flags in front of them...or a gun."

"I'd notice if she'd gotten fat."

Her mother-in-law ignored him. "Sara? You haven't answered my question."

"Actually, I think I will have some pie," she said, concentrating on cutting herself a piece.

"Good," Gertrude looked satisfied.

Problem solved. For now....

LATER THAT NIGHT she sat in front of her glowing laptop, her fingers hovering above the keyboard. There was a time not so long ago when she'd looked forward to logging on to her e-mail account and checking for new messages. Rather, she'd been eager to check "Samantha's" box. But now that Eric knew who she really was, would he seek her out at her regular account? And if he did, what would she do?

"Ignore him," she whispered.

Easier said than done.

Despite the awkward moments with her in-laws earlier, every time she turned around she was reminded of her time with Eric the other night. She hadn't changed the sheets yet because at night she snuggled into the side he'd slept on, crushing his pillow to her nose, absorbing the scent of sandalwood and hot male.

He'd tried calling, but she'd had the answering machine on. His first two attempts he'd merely hung up.

On the third, he'd left a message: "Sara, call me, please. You and I need to talk."

What was there possibly to say? She'd made a mistake. A mammoth mistake. And while there was no taking it back, she did have a say on whether or not it continued.

Sara drew a deep breath and entered her password. She clicked on the mail button and scanned the contents. A couple of spams, an e-mail from a cousin in California and…nothing.

She squinted at the screen, sure she was seeing things.

She deleted the spam, then opened her cousin's e-mail, which was essentially a vent about work.

"I hear you. Some days are a bitch to get through," she wrote back. "I—"

An instant message popped up in the middle of her screen, scaring the daylights out of her.

Sara stared at a screen name she'd come to know very well over the past few months.

Armstrong3001 had written a simple: "Hey."

She swallowed hard, trying to decide whether she should respond or to shut down the feature.

Before she knew that's what she was going to do, she typed back: "Hey, yourself."

She sat staring at the blinking cursor in the message box until her eyes grew dry and she had to blink.

What did Eric want? She'd been both afraid and hopeful that he would seek her out again. After the other morning, she wouldn't blame him if he didn't want to speak to her again. After the other morning, she was afraid she'd eagerly welcome a repeat if he offered it.

She remembered her mother-in-law holding the photo of Andy earlier and guilt settled around her shoulders like a heavy cloak.

Sara began to shut the laptop when the IM chimed and Eric's response appeared.

"I can't forget about the other night."

The frank admission caught her off guard and her hand slowly dropped from the monitor as if of its own accord.

Although she was reluctant to admit it, her every other thought was about how nice it had been to be held by him.

The problem lay in that the other thoughts were about her betrayal of the memory of her husband.

"It seems like every time I take a breath, I smell you…"

Sara gave an eye roll.

"I swear I detect the scent of lavender and vanilla everywhere. Then I remember that it's not around me now, but rather a memory of you."

Her soap and bath oil.

Okay, so it would have been easy to dismiss his initial words as so much hype, but his specific mention of her fragrance told her he was being genuine.

Of course, if she overlooked the part of her brain that told her that any contact with Eric was a bad idea, she would have recognized his honesty. Would never have questioned his sincerity. It was those qualities that had captured her attention and had drawn her to him time and again when she needed to feel connected to someone not her in-laws or work associates.

Someone who would be as honest with her as she was with him.

Her heart beat a steady, heady rhythm in her chest.

"You're more beautiful than I ever dared to imagine Samantha might be," he wrote. "More than just physical…although I loved touching you."

She swallowed hard, captivated by his words.

"There's a vulnerability about you, Sara. Yet you're

fearless when it comes to something that you want. The combination fascinates me. You fascinate me."

She caressed the keyboard with her fingertips, but the words refused to come.

"Your skin…"

Her pulse hummed.

"You're so soft. Softer than anything I've ever had the privilege to touch before…."

When they'd traded e-mails and IMs before his return, their sexy posts had been almost carnal in nature. Now there rang an emotional edge that reached out for her more powerfully than his hands.

"I loved making love to you…. Hearing your quiet gasps…your low moans… You felt so good wrapped around me. Tight… Wet… Then there was your mouth…"

Sara found her lips were parched and she ran her tongue over them as if in preparation for his kiss. Only he wasn't here. He was probably back at the base writing to her on his laptop.

"I want to touch myself right now just thinking about it, Sara. Just thinking about you…."

He might want to, but she was.

Sara found that her right hand had moved to rest against her neck. Right there, just below her ear, where he had kissed her, driving her insane with desire. She slowly trailed her fingers down over her opposite shoulder, feeling her bra strap under her T-shirt. She reached back and unfastened the confining material, letting it bow open, but not removing it.

"Your breasts…"

Yes…her breasts. She ran her palm over her right one, the nipple already drawn taut and achy.

"I could have kissed your breasts forever and never wanted for anything more…."

Sara wet her fingertips and lightly pinched her nipple, gasping as she imagined it was Eric's hand against her rather than her own.

"Then there was the surprise waiting down below…"

Sara's breath caught as she remembered him tugging her underpants down and gazing at her bare flesh. She'd started waxing when she was in her early twenties and had never really stopped, liking the feel of the clean skin against the sheets…against a man.

"I remember how ready you were for me…how engorged…"

She popped the button on her jeans and dipped her fingers inside the waistband, touching her swollen flesh through her panties first, then burrowing inside so that she caressed her hot, sensitive flesh.

"You were so wet…so ready…"

She was now, too. Oh, so ready.

"And you tasted like pure honey warmed by the summer sun…"

She dipped her index finger inside her sex and her own juices coated her skin. She pulled it out and fondled her clit, drawing small, wet circles even as she continued reading his posts through half-lidded eyes.

"But nothing compares to the moment I first entered you…"

Sweet Jesus…

"Feeling your body surrounding me, squeezing me…I've never felt for another woman what I felt in that one moment…"

Sara stiffened her first two fingers and slid them into her moist heat. But two wouldn't do. Not when Eric had filled her so thickly. She added a finger and thrust them up into her wetness.

"Knowing you were so hot for me made me feel like

I was burning up from the inside out…. And then you moved your hips…. I had to grab your bottom and hold on for dear life I was so afraid I was going to come right there and then…."

Sara shivered all over, running her tongue along her lips restlessly, longing to stretch out on the bed behind her but not daring to miss one word Eric was typing.

"I want you again, Sara… Now. Please let me in… Invite me over."

"Come…please," she wrote.

5

ERIC COULDN'T BELIEVE he'd written what he had. But once it was out, there was no taking it back. Nor, he realized, did he want to.

On the front line, there was no room for hesitation or second-guessing. To do either was to risk being killed. And after two days of torturing himself over Sara's odd behavior, he'd come to recognize that they were at a standoff of sorts. Not on a professional battlefield, but on a personal one. And he needed to pull out all the stops if he had any chance of winning this challenge.

Of course, he'd never expected Sara to accept.

But he certainly didn't plan to give her a chance to change her mind.

What would he do if she did change her mind? He'd spent so much time fantasizing about "Samantha" that he hadn't really adjusted to the fact that she was actually Sara. But somehow everything just clicked the instant he'd stood in front of her on that beach. He'd felt as if he'd known her. Not just over the past few years through his friendship with Andy, but for his entire life.

And he wanted her in his life, fair play or foul, he didn't care. He couldn't imagine a future without her in it.

He began to log off so he could drive to her place when he noticed he had an e-mail. Thinking that maybe

Sara had zipped him off something before shutting down, he double-clicked the icon to find fellow marine Matt Guerrero's name in his box.

He opened it.

"Hey. Just heard from Eddie. Court-martial is on for Brian. The date has been set for the third…"

Whatever hope that Eric felt slid off like an unbuttoned shirt.

It took Eric twenty minutes to drive to Sara's, and every minute that passed, the more he feared she'd changed her mind.

How many times over the past six months had he imagined events just like this? Feeling a need so deep, so hot, that he'd do anything in order to reach Sara?

Of course, nowhere in those imagined circumstances had she ever refused him. But now the possibility emerged a very real one, indeed.

Damn. How did he go about convincing her that his feelings were the real deal? That she needed him as much as he was coming to need her? Her stubbornness was the stuff of which wars were made. Two factions refusing to budge and meet in the middle. It was either their way or the highway. And that highway ended up being a crater-filled no-man's-land where deadly bombs were detonated and things escalated to the point where there was no truce to be had, only seething bitterness.

He didn't want that to happen with Sara. Wouldn't let it happen.

He tightened his hands on the steering wheel, understanding that he could defuse the situation himself in a simple, quick manner….

He could back out before tempers got too hot. Leave

Sara to believe that hers was the right decision. Deny his own need for her.

Not an option, he argued.

He pulled into her driveway and stalked toward her front door, determined to face whatever it was she threw his way.

Thankfully, she grabbed his arm and hauled him inside and kissed him wildly.

She hadn't changed her mind….

MASTURBATION, no matter the implements, was no comparison to the real thing.

Sara pushed a surprised Eric down onto her bed and stripped her clothes off, item by item before going to work on his until they were both nude. Then she climbed up onto the bed, straddling him in a shameless way that might have mortified her under normal conditions.

But what she was feeling was anything but normal. Her blood was on fire, raging through her body like a licking blaze, burning up every practical thought in her head. She was acting on pure instinct and fundamental desire.

And she had never felt better, more in control.

She knew that this was nothing more than an illusion. That her body's desire to mate with Eric was making her think she was in control, when actually her hormones were ruling her actions. But just then she couldn't have cared less. She just wanted to feel Eric inside her…now!

She scooted up his thighs, the springy hair there lightly scratching her as she bent to kiss him.

Eric groaned and held her head in that way that made her feel special. Like he could merely kiss her and he'd be the happiest man alive.

But she wanted more, oh, so much more.

She slid to cover his rock-hard erection between her

pulsing folds, shuddering the instant the thick knob knocked against her hypersensitive clit.

Oh, yes.

Her own fingers could never bring her this much pleasure. The pure bliss of his hot, satiny hardness against her slick softness.

She reached between them to guide him inside her, reveling in the long, thick length.

"Whoa," Eric whispered roughly. "Hold on a second while I get a rubber."

"Can't...wait..."

She ignored his attempts to stop her as she sank down over him, inch by delectable inch, taking him in.

He groaned and stopped fighting. Both of them stayed like that for a long moment, unmoving, absorbing every sweet sensation created by their joined bodies.

Sara swore she could feel her heart beating in every part of her body. Almost as if her body *was* her heart. One giant, pulsing organ capable of nothing but pure emotion. It was almost impossible for her to catch her breath.

Eric's hips bucked as if involuntarily and sheer ecstasy rocketed through her.

Yes...

Bracing her palms against his wide shoulders, she tilted her own hips forward, then back, drenching him in her essence....

ERIC COULDN'T remember the last time he'd felt a woman's flesh without the barrier of a condom.

A voice at the back of his head told him he should stop, sheath himself, protect her. But, Lord forgive him, he was incapable of doing anything that would impede the scintillating heat running over him in spectacular waves.

Was this really Sara stroking him with her body, her breasts swaying, her face a sketch of heaven?

God, but at this moment she was so beautiful she stole his breath away. She was a goddess who knew what she wanted and wasn't afraid of going about getting it, land mines and lists of demands be damned. This wasn't a truce, this was a coming together that transcended differences and preconceptions and flew up so high that the road that divided them was no longer visible.

Eric closed his eyes and ground his back teeth together to keep himself from coming too fast. She felt good. So good.

He grasped her hips and edged his fingers inward toward the bare flesh between her legs until both his thumbs slid into her shallow channel, finding the tight bud at the apex.

Sara gasped and arched her back, her breathing erratic, her stomach trembling. Eric knew that all he'd have to do was blow on her sensitive skin and she'd shatter into a million crystalline pieces. But he knew a fear that when he did that, she'd also wake up from whatever sensual haze she'd surrendered to and go back to the woman who refused to let him into her house, much less her heart.

So he moved his thumbs and fastened his roving fingers to her hips. Her tiny sound of disapproval was followed by another gasp as he thrust upward. He wanted to make this as long as he could. To claim her on a level that would be almost impossible to ignore or push away. He wanted her to remember him, to know that only he was capable of giving her this much pleasure.

A groan rose in his throat. Of course, he was forgetting that the woman absolutely wrecked him. She could have been Mata Hari demanding to know every last secret he'd ever been trusted with and he would have told her. Standing above him in dominatrix boots holding a whip and he would have begged her to lash him. Anything to keep her near. Anything to stop her from pushing him away.

He recognized her low moan and realized she was on the crux of orgasm. He tightened his grip on her hips and instantly rolled her over off him. Her sound of protest was loud and not very ladylike.

Eric grinned as he repositioned her on the bed next to him. If he had any hope of holding off his own climax, he needed to impose as much control as possible. So he turned her to her stomach and hauled her hips back so that she was on all fours. Then he nestled himself between her smooth bottom cheeks and parted her farther, baring every sweet inch of her to his hungry gaze.

He was determined that this time when she came, he would come with her….

SARA WOKE IN THE middle of the night feeling sated and sore…and more than a little remorseful.

Eric lay next to her, his soft snores telling her he was asleep, but not deeply. She slowly shifted to get out of bed only to be kept in place by Eric's arms where he held her. The snores had stopped.

"Where are you going?" he said quietly.

She swallowed thickly. "Bathroom."

"You just went."

He had her there.

She debated on whether to fight him, to insist that she had to go again. But she was too exhausted to do anything more than melt back against him despite the arguments ringing through her brain.

She felt his lips against the top of her head. "Please... don't do this again."

Guilt piled on top of Sara's entire body.

"Please don't pull away from me."

She searched for words to tell him. To explain what was happening inside her mind.

Instead she found the strength to draw away. She sat on the side of the bed, but forced herself to stay there instead of run for the door to the bathroom like she wanted to.

The bedsheets rustled and she looked over her shoulder to watch Eric lift himself up onto one arm, propping his handsome head on his hand.

"I want you to come to Texas with me," he said.

She squinted at him in the darkness. "What?"

Her heart beat a million miles a minute.

"I need to go down to take care of some things at the ranch before I leave again for Afghanistan. Come with me."

Sara's eyes burned as she pulled the top sheet up to cover herself as best she could. "I can't."

"Why?"

There was the question she'd been dreading. The one she'd been running full out from since the moment she'd first spotted him on the beach. The one she'd known was on the tip of his tongue since he'd figured out she was Samantha and that he didn't care, he wanted her anyway.

"Sara..."

She told her feet to move, but they refused her.

"I know that you think you're betraying Andy by being with me, but..."

She shifted to look at him in the darkness, the only

light in the room provided by the full moon looming large outside the bedroom window.

"Hey, look, I loved the guy, too, you know?" He ran his free hand restlessly over his close-cropped hair. "You don't think there's a day goes by that I don't wish I could have done something more to save him?" He looked everywhere but at her. His voice dropped lower. "You don't think there's a moment when I don't wish that it had been me instead of him?"

Sara's eyes burned and she bit her bottom lip to keep from making a sound.

"But that's not what went down. No matter how much I wish differently, Andy's still gone…."

She absently budged her wedding ring around her finger, seeing no more than a blur through her tears.

"But you're here, Sara." Eric reached out and touched her. "I'm here…."

6

ERIC HADN'T FELT SO convinced of something since he'd first signed on to become a marine. He knew down to his boots that asking Sara to come with him to Texas was the right thing to do. He needed her to take a step outside the past she held on to like a cocoon. Needed for her to see him as something other than an enemy and her late husband's best friend.

He needed her to see him.

He could tell this battle was going to be all uphill. With potentially no end to the hill.

He reached out and touched her bare shoulder, marveling at the satiny feel of her skin.

"Sara, I'm not asking you to marry me. At least not yet."

She shifted to stare at him so quickly that he was afraid she might fall off the side of the bed.

He grinned. "Yeah, I've thought about it. As a marine, I know that around every corner, behind every bush, someone may lurk, someone determined to end my life…I don't have to explain it to you. You've lived long enough around marines to know that we tend to have a different view of time clocks. What might loom too soon for some seems too late to a marine."

"But don't you see…that's what I'm afraid of. I've already lost one man…I couldn't go on, couldn't survive if I lost you, too…" Her words drifted off.

Eric had fully expected her to shut him out. To counter his proposal with an offensive that would leave him bleeding his emotions all over the sheets.

Instead she'd finally laid her heart, her fears, open to him.

He sat up, for the first time hope emerging, pushing through his array of weapons.

"You won't lose me, Sara. I won't allow that to happen."

"How can you say that?" she whispered. "You don't know what might happen tomorrow, or the day after that."

"Neither do you." He longed to haul her into his arms. "So why waste time we can spend together worrying about what if?"

She looked at him. The pain shining bright in her eyes sliced like a knife through his heart. "What about my job? Truman?"

He knew a strong relief. But also knew he had to act fast, before she shut him out again. "Take some time off. You can probably see to a lot of your tasks on your laptop, right? And we can take the Lab with us."

She didn't appear convinced, as if she'd expected a different answer. Or perhaps it wasn't the answer at all, but the question that should have been different.

"What about Gertrude and Howard?"

Andy's parents.

Eric blinked. In all honesty, he had never considered the older couple. Andy had been their only child. And when he'd visited the other day, he couldn't help feeling awkward in their company. Because of the circumstances of his past with Andy, yes, but there had been something more…almost as if their continued close connection with Sara allowed them to buy into the delusion that their son was only away on assignment and he would be returning any day now.

"Tell them you're going on vacation."

She laughed without humor. "I never go on vacation."

He reached out and cupped her chin with his hand, wiping some of the dampness from her skin. "Well, then, it sounds like it's long time since you started…."

To his surprise, she leaned into his touch and then melted into his arms, allowing the sheet to drop. Eric closed his eyes, marveling in the warmth of her skin against his. How small. How sexy.

Her movements doubled the hope swelling inside him. Did he finally have her? Would she come to Texas with him?

He thought of his family and all he'd introduce to her. Show her. From the stables to the back nine where he used to spend so much of his time as a kid chewing on stalks of straw and contemplating the world from under his Oilers ball cap.

"I can't."

She'd said the words so quietly, he nearly didn't hear them.

But hear them, he did. And his heart dipped low in his stomach. But rather than let go of her, he held her closer.

"Thank you, Eric. Your offer is the best one I've heard in a long, long time."

He heard the deep click of her swallow even as she clutched him like she might never let him go, despite the meaning of her words.

"But I can't."

He tried to open his mouth, push out the word sitting on the tip of his tongue: *Why?* But it refused to come. Mostly because he didn't have a breath on which it could exit.

She pulled slightly away, searching his face in the dim light. "I have so much to thank you for. For being patient. For making me feel alive again when I'd felt like I'd died right along with Andy. For...well, for making me look to the future again with curiosity rather than dread."

"Then come to Texas with me, Sara. Take that step into the future."

She looked down and slowly shook her head. "I understand that you have your timetable, Eric. What you must understand is that I also have one. And it has yet to adjust to all the changes you've wrought in my life in the past week." She blinked up again and caressed the side of his face much as he'd done to her moments before. "I can't move at your pace. Too many people will get hurt if I do." She smiled a ghost of a smile. "Including me."

"I'd never hurt you."

"No, you wouldn't. At least not purposely."

He opened his mouth to protest and she rested her hand against his lips.

"Shhh. I'm not done yet."

He forced himself to shut up and listen.

"I need you to promise me something."

He wanted to say he'd do anything she wanted. Then he realized that this particular promise was going to be something he didn't like.

"I want you to promise that when you leave here tomorrow morning, that you do so without looking back." Her voice caught and she appeared to have trouble keeping her breathing even. "I want...no, need you to promise me that you won't try to contact me. Not by phone. Not by e-mail. Not by IM. Not by any means."

"Sara—"

"Promise me, Eric."

He drew her close again and she rested her cheek against his shoulder, holding him just as tightly.

It was all so confusing.

If she was admitting that she wanted him, with both her words and her body, then why was she still pushing him away?

"I can't," he whispered fiercely into her hair, holding a fist full of it gently. "I can't imagine not being able to see you, Sara. Not being able to talk to you."

She made a small sound as she kissed his arm. "Who said you wouldn't be doing either?"

"But how…"

He stopped.

"If this is going to happen, I have to be in control. If you force me into it, I may end up regretting it later. Regretting you. And I don't want to do that."

He didn't want that to happen, either.

But he couldn't stand the idea that he would have no sway over her. Didn't trust that the moment he walked out of her front door that she wouldn't go back to being Andy's widow and lock herself out from the world all over again.

"Promise me," she whispered, pulling away to stare intently up into his face.

In that one moment he would have promised her anything. Even if it meant severing one of his own limbs.

"I promise," he said.

7

THREE DAYS LATER, Sara wandered through the house touching objects, picking them up, putting them back down. Never had she experienced the sensation of being adrift. Unsure of who she was and what she was doing. Everything had always emerged so clear.

Now...

Well, now she was waiting for her mother-in-law to arrive for an impromptu cup of coffee.

She'd called Gertrude an hour ago and invited her over, surprising them both with the spontaneous invitation. She'd half expected her mother-in-law to bow out, postpone the meeting because Sara knew she played bridge around this time every week.

But Gert had readily accepted.

Truman whined and she looked down at him. He appeared to be eyeing a photo she held of Andy and him taken at the beach so many years before. The same photo Gertrude picked up every time she visited.

She didn't know what she was going to say exactly. She just knew she had to say something. Perhaps she'd begin with the fact that she hated the symphony.

No. That would be too cruel. She couldn't do this all at once. She couldn't bring herself to break Gertrude's heart along with her own.

And that's what it felt like, didn't it? Like her heart was breaking all over again.

There was a light knock at the door. Sara put the photo back down on the dining-room sideboard. She wiped her damp palms on her jeans as she went to open it.

"Is everything all right, Sara?" Gertrude asked, breezing into the room on a cloud of Chanel No. 5.

Sara accepted her hug and returned it.

"Yes, yes. Sorry, I didn't mean to concern you. Everything's fine."

Or at least they were on their way to being fine.

"Actually," she began, and haltingly explained about what had happened in the past week.

Surprisingly, it didn't take long. What had seemed like a capital crime to her sounded like a minor offense once it was out in the open.

She finished on a soft exhale and then sat, waiting for her mother-in-law's response.

"Oh, thank God!" Gertrude said.

Sara blinked at her. "What?" she whispered.

"Oh, dear girl. All this time you thought that Howard and I would be disappointed if you finally moved on? For heaven's sake, your emotional well-being has been topic number one in our home for at least the past year. You've seemed…I don't know, so incapable of moving on. Like you were stuck in the past…."

Sara couldn't believe she was hearing what she was. Was it possible that she'd gotten it wrong?

Or worse yet, had she clutched onto her in-laws as the reason she kept the house exactly the same, lived every moment like Andy had just left the day before, when all along it had been she who had been incapable of moving on?

The possibility made her dizzy.

"Howard was just saying that maybe I should suggest you should meet with a therapist from the base. Someone to help you through in a way that apparently we were unable to…."

Sara not so much as sat down in Andy's old recliner as she collapsed into it, covering her face with her hands.

"Oh, God. I'm sorry, Sara. See, this is exactly what we didn't want to cause. Here, take a tissue."

Sara looked up at where Gertrude was offering a box of Kleenex. She wasn't crying, she was laughing.

Which only confused the other woman more.

She did accept a tissue, only the dampness on her cheeks had nothing to do with pain.

"What a mess we've all made of things," she said.

"Of course, Howard and I hope you'll stay in contact. You're the closest thing that we have to a child."

Sara stood up and hugged her tightly. "Just you try getting rid of me."

Gertrude tucked her hair behind her ear. A gesture a mother might make to a much younger child.

"There is one small thing…" Sara began.

"Anything, sweetie. Anything."

"I hate the symphony."

Laughter sparkled in Gertrude's eyes. "Maybe we should set some parameters pertaining to this new openness…"

THE SUN ROSE LIKE A pale orange ball over the horizon, kissing the West Texas landscape like an indifferent lover. Eric brought his stallion around, nudging him toward the stables.

Five days had passed since he'd made that promise to Sara. Five days since he'd gazed into her beautiful eyes. Five days since he'd attempted to take his fill of her body.

And he was slowly coming to understand that she'd done what he'd feared she would: She had used his promise as a way to go back to her cold, empty shell of a life.

And had condemned him to his.

He tugged a little too hard on the reins and Skywalker neighed in protest.

"Sorry, buddy," he said, patting the stallion's shiny black neck.

Damn him and his word. If he knew what was good for him, he'd fly right back up to Virginia Beach and ravish Sara until she had no choice but to change her mind.

But if there was one thing he'd been taught, first as a member of the Armstrong clan, then as a United States marine, it was that a man was only as good as his word. Once you took away all the money and the trappings, all that remained was what a man said, what a man did. And that was the most valuable commodity of all. It was something that couldn't be bought, couldn't be traded. A man was a man or he wasn't. That was that. No two ways about it.

He brought Sky to a stop and climbed from the majestic beast, catching notice of the way the ranch hands warily eyed him as they exited their quarters a few hundred feet behind the stables. He gave a brief wave. They touched the rim of their hats or waved back.

Truth was, he'd been little good around the place since his return. Like last night, he'd been unable to sleep and found himself saddling up Skywalker long before dawn and taking him out for a ride meant to clear his head. He kept waiting for the lack of sleep to catch up to him, but so far there was no sign of that happening. Well, beyond the screwups he'd made around the ranch, which were legendary.

Even his younger brother had threatened to buy him a first-class ticket back to Iraq first thing tomorrow if he didn't straighten up and fly right. And he believed him.

He shook his head, unable to believe that his brother had grown so much in the time he'd been away. Trace had gone from gangly, sulky teen to hulking, commanding man overnight. Or so it seemed.

One of the horses had taken ill the night before and he'd called in the vet. He hoped it was nothing more than an intestinal bug.

Dust kicked up in the distance, announcing the arrival of someone via the back road. He squinted, trying to make out the Doc Trane's truck. The vehicle was red, all right…except it wasn't a truck, but rather one of those subcompact cars you rarely saw in this part of Texas. He was amazed it managed to stay on the road as its little donut tires bumped against the rutted track.

"Probably one of those Jesus freaks comin' out with that literature they're always pressing into your hands," Trace said next to him.

Eric pushed his hat back on his head. "Maybe."

Still, he allowed himself to indulge in that hope with which he'd become all too familiar in Virginia Beach. It was the same feeling he got every time the phone rang, or an e-mail popped up in his box.

Or whenever an unknown car pulled up the road.

"Eric?"

He glanced at Trace without really seeing him. "You and the guys go on ahead. I'll catch up…." he said quietly.

"Sure thing."

He barely registered the sound of Trace's horse's hooves as he steered him away. A wolf whistle later and the cattle were being hustled from the corral and ushered out onto the range.

But all Eric could see was the dot of the approaching car as it grew larger.

Sky neighed and he absently patted his neck as he passed off the reins to the stableboy who'd hurried out at his call.

The car was finally near enough to make out. The plates read Texas, but he had the feeling that the driver was from anywhere but, and had likely taken out an axel on his or her approach. The sides were covered with dust, nearly blotting out the bright color. Eric took off his hat and shaded his eyes with his hand.

His heart nearly dropped to the dirt at his feet as the woman climbed from behind the wheel. She stood next to open door as if in a trance....

Sara...

Eric hadn't known he'd moved until he found Sara in his arms, lifting her off her feet and squeezing her so hard she probably couldn't breathe. Her breasts pressed against the wall of his chest, her softness rested against his instant hardness.

Her laughter rang in his ears.

"I wasn't sure I'd still be welcome," she said into his ear.

He put her down on her feet and stood staring down at her, trying to discern if this was a dream or reality. In that one moment, he didn't care. Just so he never awakened.

"You came," he said in wonder.

Her smile competed with the rising sun and won. "I came."

He couldn't quite bring himself to believe it. He'd just managed to convince himself that it was over. Whatever they had would go no further. Yet now she stood in front of him looking as nervous as a filly facing her first stallion. The reaction was new to him. And in return, he didn't quite know how to react himself.

She looked around and he thought that an introduction to the place might be a good idea. But he couldn't seem to stop staring at her, dumbfounded.

She cleared her throat. "I have to warn you…I don't know if I'm ready for this…ready for you."

He didn't care. Just so long as she was here. He knew what it must have taken for her to get on that plane and see through what easily had to be a ten-hour trip once you factored in connection and drive times, giving her all sorts of opportunities to turn back.

She took a deep breath. "I promised myself I wasn't going to do this," she said.

"Do what?"

"Ramble."

God, but she had to be the sexiest thing he'd ever laid eyes on.

She took him in from head to foot, apparently approving of his chaps and hat.

"Okay, let's just start over.…"

Then she thrust her hand toward him.

Eric considered the outstretched limb. The hand that had held him, cradled him, brought him so much pleasure.

"Hi. My name's Sara Harris. And I'd love to go out with you."

Eric raised a brow. Go out with him? They'd already been to home plate and back.

He grinned. "Hi, Sara Harris. I'm Eric Armstrong. And I'd love to take you out."

As he held her hand in his, he knew that he would do everything in his power to make sure she never left.…

Eddie

1

MARINE LANCE CORPORAL Eddie Cash's mother had often told him that he would never amount to much.

Eddie never really let her words bother him. He knew she hadn't meant them in an insulting way. They were said with as much passion as "the media will never understand what we common folk go through," or "the sky's red this morning, you better take your umbrella." They were statements of facts as she saw them, nothing more, nothing less.

As the only child of Trixie McGee, he had come to understand that she didn't know any better. And that she'd been shaped by life experiences that had included a man who had fathered her baby and then gone and gotten himself killed, a lifetime of waiting tables at the diner in the small town in of Parkers Creek, North Carolina—a diner not unlike the restaurant he now sat in—and an extended family that counted only one high-school grad in their midst: ironically, Simple Eddie.

It didn't bother him that his mother never acknowledged what he did around the house, how by age fifteen he was already contributing more to their overhead than she was or how he always made sure she had her little creature comforts like her chamomile tea and soaking salts.

Of course, he knew that part of the reason why he

didn't hold a grudge was that she'd died two years ago. Doc Johnson had said she'd gone quietly sitting in her recliner watching her stories. No, no one knew she'd had a heart problem, but then again, few in Eddie's family actually went to the doctor when they were sick, much less for regular visits. It's just the way things went. When you didn't know if you were going to be able to pay the light bill that month, little things like the pain in your arm or the dizziness you felt when you stood up too fast were easy to explain away as hazards of the job or lack of proper nutrition.

"I've probably got that diabetes," his mother had told him on the phone a short time before she passed.

He'd had no reason to question her. Merely told her it would probably be a good idea to get her blood checked. She'd told him there was one of those traveling free clinic deals coming through town in a couple of months, maybe she'd go stand in line and get it done then.

She'd never made it to the clinic.

"Would you like to hear the specials?" the familiar waitress asked, looking harried as she nearly leaned against his table.

She didn't recognize him. Not surprising because she had yet to look directly at him.

Damn, but she was as pretty as she'd ever been.

He cleared his throat, "I think I'll have a big slice of your peach cobbler."

There was a heartbeat of a pause, then the color seemed to drain out of her already pale face. She slowly looked up from her pad, staring at him as if he'd dropped straight out of the sky and landed in her workstation.

"Eddie!" Megan Walker's hand immediately went

to the neck of her pink, ruffled uniform. There was a spot on the bottom right corner of her white apron. Coffee, probably. Maybe gravy. Whatever it was, he imagined her at the kitchen sink at home trying to scrub it out later that night, no matter how tired she was.

His gaze drifted down over breasts that were even fuller now, and lower still to where her stomach curved around the baby she carried. Their baby.

She was six months and two days pregnant. He could calculate the time straight down to the minute. Trail it back to that hot July night when he'd come into the restaurant after drinking with the boys, and she'd been turning the Closed sign.

He'd talked her into letting him in to get a piece of peach cobbler that he later found out she'd made, and then seduced her into letting him trail his hand up her frilly, silly little skirt into forbidden areas. She'd opened to him like one of the roses in his mother's backyard.

And introduced him to dozens of different scents and colors over the two weeks that remained during his leave.

He couldn't have been more surprised when she'd tracked him down through some contact service and sent him a letter telling him she was pregnant.

"I didn't know you were on leave," she said now, looking over her shoulder.

The place hadn't gotten any less busy, but somehow Eddie felt as if it had emptied out. There was only him and the soon-to-be mother of his child.

"I'm not out on leave."

She squinted at him.

"I'm out."

He couldn't identify her reaction. Part sadness, part exasperation?

"We're all out of cobbler." She turned and walked away.

Eddie watched after her, puzzled.

After he'd received her letter months earlier, he'd called her at the number he'd kept tucked behind his driver's license in his wallet. She'd told him basically the same thing she had in her letter: she was having the baby and just thought he should know. The conversation had been brief. But Eddie had called again. Only to get her voice mail. "It's Eddie. I'll call back."

Sometimes he got her and she'd share what the doctor had said, how the pregnancy was progressing, but mostly he got her voice mail.

Another waitress came to the table. "Would you like to hear the specials?"

He half listened to the options, telling her he would take the first one, which happened to be an open roast beef sandwich with mashed potatoes and gravy. Which was fine with him. He'd never been picky about what he ate.

Anyway, he wasn't there for the food.

He'd purposely come at the tail end of the dinner crowd, hoping to wait around until Megan got off. He'd figured this would be the best. He wasn't sure how she'd take him just showing up at her apartment.

He took his time with the meal and then followed up with a piece of apple pie and coffee. The crowd finally began thinning out. He saw Megan standing at the counter, her hands braced against her lower back as she talked to another waitress. He'd felt her looking at him several times, but whenever he'd tried to meet her gaze, she'd quickly pretended she'd been doing something else.

"Hi!" A young woman in the booth behind him tapped him on the arm. "My friend here and I have a bet.

She says you're in the army. I say the air force. Which one of us is right?"

"Neither. I'm a marine."

"Oh, a marine. Aren't they, like, the toughest ones in the military?" the friend asked.

"We like to think so."

The first one got up and slid in the seat opposite him. "Mind if we join you? We noticed you're eating alone. And since we're alone, too…well, why don't we all be alone together?"

Eddie barely heard her. His gaze was fastened on where Megan had gathered her personal items from the back room and was heading toward the front door.

"If you'll excuse me," he said to his uninvited guests. He stopped at the register and gave the cashier enough money to cover his bill and anything the two women might order, then hurried after Megan.

"Meggie!" he called.

She'd already walked across the parking lot in the direction of the street. She slowed her step but didn't turn.

"Where's your car?" he asked.

She finally stopped. "It broke down the day before yesterday. The mechanic says I need a new alternator."

He looked in the direction of the apartment building she lived in with her mother, a good two miles down the road. "You've been walking?"

"Of course, I've been walking. I can't magically sprout wings and fly."

He smiled. "How about I give you a ride?"

She looked around, as if trying to determine which car was his out of the seven or so that remained, or for someone else to rescue her—he wasn't sure which.

Finally she sighed. "Normally I wouldn't accept a ride from a stranger, but my feet are killing me."

DESPITE HER ACHING feet and back, Megan couldn't help noticing that there were a few details she'd forgotten about the hot marine who, six months ago, had romanced her into the state she was now in. Beginning with how tall he was. And how muscular. And handsome.

Of course, it had taken a lot more than that to hold her captivated. She'd never been the type to mess around with every attractive guy that crossed her path and she'd been surprised when she'd slept with Eddie Cash on the first night she'd met him.

Somewhere down the line she'd forgotten all about that as she watched her waistline expand and her bills pile up.

Oh, he'd said he'd take care of her and his baby. It had been an outdated, almost chivalrous thing to do considering she could count at least three friends who had children whose fathers didn't want anything to do with them, much less offered any kind of financial support. At least she could say that for Eddie. He'd never even asked if the baby was his, as she'd expected him to, either. Never demanded a DNA test. Never even asked if there was anyone else. He'd merely inquired as to how she was feeling and sent her a check. Then another one. Until she received one once a month like clockwork.

Even her mother, as jaded as she was, had been surprised. "Usually you have to drag their sorry asses into court and have support ordered," she'd said upon receipt of the third check.

Megan hadn't pointed out that she had yet to have the baby, so the money couldn't even be considered child support. She received all her health care free from the clinic in Fayetteville thirty miles away and had enrolled in a Medicare program to see her through the delivery.

She'd prefer to have a job that provided health care, but the restaurant only paid waitstaff half of minimum wage and didn't offer insurance except to the managerial staff. The larger percent of their income came in tips. Which meant on a slow night she was lucky to come up with thirty to forty dollars, which barely covered the gas she needed to get back and forth to work, considering she drove a fifteen-year-old Crown Victoria with over two hundred thousand miles on it.

Sometimes late at night, she'd lie in bed wondering if she'd made the right decision. What kind of life was she going to be able to give this baby? The type of life she'd had? Her mother had worked in the textile factory up until six years ago when she'd taken a buyout. The money she'd gotten had lasted two years and then Becky Sue had gone to work as a cashier at a gun supply shop that paid her ten percent of what she used to get.

Megan couldn't remember a time when they hadn't had to struggle.

And now she was repeating her mother's mistakes.

She looked over at Eddie. At least her baby would know who her father was.

"You never did talk much, did you?" she said quietly.

He was driving slowly. Perhaps a little too slowly. As if trying to work something out that took all of his concentration. "I'm still wondering why you called me a stranger."

Megan looked out of the passenger window of the old truck. "Well, that's what you are, aren't you? Six months ago, neither one of us made much of effort to get to know each other beyond the bedroom."

Her cheeks felt hot at the admission. Or rather the memory of those hot, summer days filled with low groans and soft cries. She'd never physically wanted a man so much in her life. Not just once, but twice, and a third time, until they'd spent nearly every waking moment of his leave with their limbs entangled.

Then he'd left and two weeks after that she'd discovered why condoms weren't considered one hundred percent effective.

Did he think about those days and nights the same way she did? Or were they merely a blip on his military radar?

She realized she hadn't told him she still lived with her mother only to see that she hadn't needed to—he was pulling into the apartment complex where they lived.

The three separate buildings dated back to the sixties and were in need of major updating, but it had been home to Megan and her mother for the past ten years.

She climbed out of the truck and pulled her cardigan a little closer.

"Which one's your car?" Eddie asked.

Megan pointed to the Crown Victoria a few parking spots away, looking at the sorry excuse for a car. Her mother's wasn't much better. An old Mazda that had been stripped by the previous owner of all the seats save for the driver's. And that one was so beat up, the cracked plastic covering bit into Megan's legs no matter how many towels she folded on top of it.

"So…" she began, standing near the walkway that would take her to her building.

Eddie was watching her closely. A little too closely.

He smelled good. Like tangy lime and deodorant soap.

To Megan's surprise, her mouth watered.

As if reading her mind, Eddie stepped forward and kissed her.

She didn't have time to protest. Barely had the time

to register what he was doing before he pulled away again, grinning at her.

It had been a good long time since she'd been kissed, much less kissed properly. And she wasn't about to let this opportunity pass.

Megan leaned in toward him and near about devoured him....

2

WAS IT NORMAL FOR A six-month pregnant woman to be horny?

The following morning Megan absently soaped up her plump belly in the shower, running the bar of soap up and down, then down a little farther. She remembered the hungry feel of Eddie's mouth against hers the night before and gasped when the soap met with the tangle of curls at the apex of her thighs.

Holy cow…

She couldn't recall a single moment in the past six months when she'd felt physically aware of her body outside of her pregnancy. And now…now she was sure if she slid her fingers into the shallow crevice between her legs she'd come instantly.

There was an insistent knock on the bathroom door and the handle jangled. "Lord, girl, what you going and locking the door on me for?"

Megan started, only partially aware that she had pushed in the lock on the old door when she'd come in to take her shower.

"Just a second," she called out, curious to find her mouth dry even as she was being bombarded by water.

She shut off the shower and reached for a towel only to watch as her mother barged inside, a knitting needle in hand that she'd used to pop the lock from the other side.

"I've got to go so bad my eyes are turning yellow," her mother said, pulling her elastic-topped polyester pants down and sitting on the toilet, blocking Megan inside the tub.

She concentrated on drying herself.

"Why is it that you don't realize you have to go until someone's locked themselves in the bathroom?" her mother asked.

"Power of suggestion."

Her mother looked dubious. "You always were a little too smart for your own good." She looked at where Megan rubbed the towel over her belly, the terry cloth blocking all the private parts. "Good Lord, what are you eating?"

Megan stopped her movements and stared at her.

"I know you're pregnant, but I wasn't that big with you at six months."

"How can you remember? That was twenty-two years ago."

"Trust me, things like that you never forget."

"Whatever. Anyway, maybe it's going to be a big baby."

"Yeah," her mother said, finishing up and flushing the toilet. "Just like his father."

What did her mother remember about Eddie?

"Speaking of which, the big lug is out there trying to fix your car."

Megan froze. "What?"

"You heard me. Been out there since right after the sun came up."

Megan hurried to get out of the tub, moving her mother out of the way as she wrapped the towel around her and rushed toward the window in her tiny bedroom.

Sure enough, there stood Eddie, his back to her as he bent over the engine of her Crown Vic.

What was he doing?

"Looks to me like he's trying to fix that hunk of junk of yours," her mother said next to her.

Megan gave her a long-suffering look, unaware that she'd asked the question aloud.

Her mother made a small sound of doubt. "I took some coffee out to him about a half hour ago."

Megan gaped at her. "You did what?"

Her mother shrugged as she left the room and went into the kitchen/dining room. "Looked like he could use a cup. By the way, you could have told me he was out."

The way she said it made it sound like he could have as easily gotten out of the state pen as the service.

She didn't argue the point. "I didn't know he'd been discharged until last night. He came by the restaurant and gave me a ride home."

She rifled through her drawers, looking for something to wear. As she got bigger, her wardrobe choices shrank. Having a uniform that fit was a must, leaving her with little cash left over for everyday clothes outside roomy sweatsuits.

She pulled out a chocolate-brown velour hoody suit her mother had bought her for Christmas and said a little prayer that it still fit. When she pulled up the pants, she sighed in relief. Although why she was concerned about how she looked was beyond her. Eddie was the baby's father. Nothing more, nothing less. While they had to get along for the baby's sake, that's where their relationship began and ended.

Oh, yeah? Then why was she spritzing on her favorite musk? And why couldn't she seem to forget about last night's kiss?

She rushed out into the living room.

"Hair," her mother said from where she washed dishes.

Megan stared at her. How did her mother know these things? She wasn't even looking.

She rushed back into the bathroom and began blow-drying her hair.

AN HOUR LATER, EDDIE sat opposite Megan at a nearby diner, watching her pick at her eggs. Unfortunately, he hadn't been able to fix her car. Which might be a good thing, since he didn't think it was safe for her to be driving such a mammoth gas-guzzler anyway. It may be the alternator now, but he had a feeling the tranny was about to give, and then after that the gaskets might break, or an axel. With a car that old, you never knew what might happen.

He'd talked her into letting him take her to breakfast. He told himself it was because he wanted to make sure she was eating properly. But as he found his gaze drawn to the fullness of her breasts, and the way she bit her plump bottom lip, he knew he wasn't coping with the real reason.

Damn, but she was even more beautiful than in the single picture he had of her. They said that being pregnant made a woman glow. But it was even more than that with Megan. Her cheeks were pinker, her eyes brighter. Everything about her seemed to radiate a health he hadn't expected.

"Express an interest in her...an interest in her experiences carrying your baby...." the counselor's words echoed in his mind.

Not that he needed to be prompted for that. He wished he could have been with Megan through every step of her pregnancy.

Now he cleared his throat. "Did you have morning sickness?"

Megan blinked at him. "What?"

He chuckled as he wiped his mouth. He'd practically demolished his supersize breakfast while she'd barely touched her eggs and toast. "Sorry. That's probably not a good topic to bring up just now."

She smiled, but looked back at her plate.

"Are you feeling sick now?"

"No. Why?"

"You're not eating."

"Sorry. I don't mean for you to waste your money. I just don't feel that hungry right now."

"Don't worry about it."

She squinted at him as if expecting a different response.

"Anyway," she said, "I've never been much of a breakfast kind of girl. Coffee, mostly. But I can't drink that now." She sipped her orange juice. "Don't worry. I'll make up for the missed meal later. The baby will make sure of that."

"Are you taking vitamins?"

She nodded.

"Good."

The waitress came and Megan went out of her way to help her collect the plates. As soon as the table was clear, she leaned her forearms on the table and sat forward. "So what do you plan to do now that you're out of the service?"

"I have a couple of things lined up."

"Like what?"

"Some construction. Some landscaping."

She frowned.

God, he was fascinated by her even when she grimaced. Eddie had gotten very little sleep last night because his head had been filled with everything he wanted to do…and because every time he closed his eyes all he could see was Megan's decadent mouth.

He'd felt instantly guilty. Was he supposed to be feeling this way about the soon-to-be mother of his baby? He hadn't thought to ask the counselor about the possibility simply because it hadn't existed as one to him. Not then.

Now…

Now all he could seem to think about was peeling open her velvety jacket and taking in the breasts that pressed against the soft fabric. About placing his mouth against her protruding stomach. Of going down even farther and seeing if she still tasted like the peach cobbler that had been her specialty.

"What time do you go into work?" he asked.

She looked at her watch. "In a couple of hours. I'm working two shifts today."

"You think that's a good idea?"

"Do I think what's a good idea? That I work as many hours as I can before the baby's born?"

"So you requested the time."

"Yes. And thankfully they're giving it to me."

"What's the doctor say?"

"About my working? She says that so long as I'm feeling well, I can work right up till the delivery."

It was his turn to frown.

"It's not like I have a choice."

He stared at her intently. "I want you to know that if you need anything, and I mean anything, that all you have to do is ask."

Surprisingly, Megan reached across to cover his hand with hers. "Women have been birthing babies for as long as history, as my mother likes to say. So long as I'm healthy, there's nothing I, um, can't do."

Eddie caught the slight hitch in her voice and zoomed in on her face. Was it him, or had her pupils widened just that little bit? Had her tongue just glided around her bottom lip as if readying it for his kiss? Were her nipples hardening beneath her jacket?

"Anything?"

Megan slowly nodded her head.

And Eddie knew that he had to get her alone as soon as he possibly could....

"I WASN'T PLANNING on bringing you here until I had a chance to fix the place up a bit."

Megan looked around the small, one-story three-bedroom house, barely seeing anything beyond the haze of her heightened sexual awareness of the man who seemed to have forgotten why he'd driven her the half hour to his place.

Given his words, she expected to see discarded fast-food wrappers and beer cans littering the floor. Instead, the place was painfully clean...of everything. Aside from an old, iron double bed in the first bedroom, and a small table with two old chairs in the kitchen, the house was empty.

The only thing that concerned her was the bed.

She stepped closer to him, close enough to touch. "Remember when you said that if I needed anything, to let you know?"

He finally stopped looking around the house like it was lacking in some manner she couldn't see. "Yes."

"Well, right now I need for you to kiss me, Eddie."

He drew her into his arms, a smile curving his well-defined lips. "That's one request I'll be more than happy to grant...."

Megan's knees went limp as he moved his mouth over hers. If it were possible to elevate kissing to an art, then Eddie had mastered it and then some. Then again, she got the very strong impression that Eddie strove to excel at anything he did. She had little doubt that he was a top-rate marine and that he'd served well. Lord knew he'd taken great care of her when they'd dated six months ago, and the instant he'd found out about the baby, he'd stepped up without question, without hesitation.

She heard the zipper on her jacket and realized he'd pulled back, watching the metallic closure inch slowly downward. She swallowed thickly. She'd never had an opportunity to grow self-conscious of her growing body, probably because there hadn't been a man about to be self-conscious around. So it was puzzling to her that she suddenly felt an urge to catch his hand, to stop him from seeing her naked in the bright light of day.

"Shh...you're beautiful, Meggie."

In that one moment, she knew she'd give him anything he wanted....

3

DAMN, THIS WAS PURE torture.

Nowhere on Eddie's carefully compiled list was: seduce the mother of his child. Yet there he stood, unzipping Megan's top, hesitating when she caught his hands as if ashamed of her own body.

But now that he'd started, he didn't want to stop.

She removed his hands and he was afraid that was that. She had come to her senses before he had and was putting a halt to what should never have begun in the first place.

Eddie knew a bone-deep disappointment.

Then watched in fascination as Megan, herself, finished what he'd started, unzipping her top inch by torturous inch, her gaze plastered to his.

Her skin reminded him of the fresh whole milk his mother used to pour into a bowl for him and then sprinkle with a little sugar when he was a kid and she'd run out of money until the next paycheck. Her breasts were bigger than he remembered, made so by pregnancy. He could make out the darker circles of her areoles under her simple cotton bra. His mouth watered with the desire to pull one of the stiff nipples between his lips.

Megan kissed him.

Eddie channeled his hunger into kissing her back. He'd get to her breasts soon. Very soon.

Now he cradled her against his chest, helping her undress him even as he continued stripping her of the brown velvet, revealing the even softer skin underneath.

Until he reached her stomach…

Eddie knew a moment of such profound pause it took his breath away.

His baby.

He pulled back to look at where his hands rested on either side of her rounded stomach. It was the size of a small basketball. And surprisingly, just as hard.

"She kicks sometimes."

He looked up into her face. "She?"

Megan smiled. "Or he. But for some reason I always refer to her as a she. I…I decided I didn't want to know the sex. So many of life's mysteries have been stripped away. I wanted to hold on to this one."

Her admission touched him in places he hadn't known existed.

He smoothed his fingers over her belly, down and back up, remembering what he'd read. He longed to be the one to apply cocoa butter to the stretched skin, massage it. He'd even bought a bottle that sat in the bathroom, but he didn't dare go to get it, too afraid that if he made the wrong move, said the wrong thing, Megan might put her jacket back on.

He budged his fingers down farther south, touching the top of her damp curls. Megan's gasp made him forget everything except that he wanted to make love to her so badly he ached.

He drew her closer again, skin against skin.

"Are you sure this is okay?" he asked.

She swallowed hard, absently rubbing her hips against his rock-hard erection. "I can have sex until a couple of weeks before delivery."

He drew back to gaze into her lush green eyes. "That's not what I was asking."

"Oh." She looked down, as if weighing his words, then her lashes swept back up, her expression full of need and certainty. "I want you to make love to me, Eddie."

That's all he needed to hear.

He carefully swept her up into his arms and carried her to his bedroom just few short feet away….

EDDIE WAS SO GENTLE and attentive that Megan thought she might burst with building passion. Every touch of his fingers against her sensitive stomach, every lap of his tongue against her distended nipples, every rub of his penis against her engorged flesh, robbed her of breath and made her feel like the woman she was. Not a hard-working waitress or an expectant mother of whom much was expected, but a flesh-and-blood woman complete with certain needs. Needs Eddie seemed so tuned in to that she might have been concerned was she not enjoying it so much.

She was surprised, however, when he put on a condom.

She rested her forehead against his. "In case you hadn't noticed, I'm already pregnant."

"That's not why I'm wearing it." He kissed her deeply. "I want to protect you and our baby."

Our baby.

For so long she had thought of her—him—in terms of being *her* baby, that the broadening of possession made her feel odd…and strangely reassured.

For the first time, she didn't feel alone in this journey. While her mother might be incredible support, she was Grandma, not an equal partner. And while she had no idea what role Eddie planned to play, in that one moment she enjoyed thinking that it would be a considerable one.

He placed the knob of his erection against her as if testing her readiness.

"Yes," she hissed, arching her back and bearing against him.

He entered her in one long, sweet stroke.

And Megan came instantly.

EDDIE WAS USED TO being the one in danger of shooting his load too soon. He'd never had a woman reach orgasm so quickly. Not that he'd known many women, but he'd been in the military long enough, where time between encounters was long and conversation was active, the men keeping very few secrets. And a common complaint was that while it appeared a woman could achieve climax immediately when she was seeing to her own needs—masturbation, Eddie guessed—it seemed to take forever for her to achieve it with a male partner.

That wasn't Eddie's experience, but he hadn't told them that. Well, okay, maybe he had. And received ribbing that he'd not been with enough women to offer up an opinion.

He gritted his teeth as Megan's tight muscles squeezed him like a slick glove. They'd change their minds if they could know about this.

Of course, none of that changed the fact that since she had climaxed so quickly, she might be done.

Her spasms subsided and she pulled him down to kiss her lingeringly. God, but she tasted so good.

He took her actions as a sign that they were done for now and began to withdraw. She instantly grabbed his hips, holding him in place.

"Where do you think you're going?" she rasped.

She rocked her hips in a way that caught him off guard and almost sent him hurling over the edge.

"We aren't anywhere near done."

He grinned and kissed her again. "I was hoping you'd say that...."

4

TWO DAYS LATER, MEGAN finished with her final lunch customer and sat down at the counter, more exhausted than she could remember feeling in a good, long time.

If part of the reason lay in that Eddie had barely said two words to her as he drove her to and from work, she wasn't ready to acknowledge it. It was almost as if they hadn't shared the intimacy they had a couple of days ago. Two hours ago, he'd said hello when he'd picked her up, then didn't speak again until he'd asked for her car keys. She'd given them to him, half expecting to find her car fixed when she got off and for Eddie to leave with nothing more than a simple goodbye.

She reached down and slid her shoe off, absently rubbing the arch with her fingers.

"Long night?" her fellow waitress Genie asked.

She frowned. "You have no idea."

"I still can't believe you slept with him. You."

Megan stiffened. "Why not me?"

Genie held her hands up. "Don't get pissy with me, missy. You're the one who's the first to shoot a guy down before he's even halfway through hello."

Genie had a point. Even before Eddie had come into her life six months ago, a man was the last thing she'd wanted. Oh, once or twice she'd picked a particularly nice-looking one for a weekend tryst to satisfy fundamental cravings, but she hadn't had a steady boyfriend since high school. She'd been too busy trying to figure out how she and her mother were going to pay next month's rent and what she wanted to do that didn't include orthopedic shoes and hairnets for the rest of her life.

Not that she'd had a chance to act on anything, but she had requested some course information online from a nearby community college last year. She'd used one of the library's computers. But aside from browsing through the glossy brochures that had arrived a few days later, she hadn't had a chance to decide on whether she wanted to train to be a dental hygienist or nurse.

Of course, both required much more schooling than she could afford in money or time, but it had been a nice thought.

God, what would she do if she woke up twenty years from now and found herself still a waitress?

She looked over at Genie and started.

"It's a living," her mother had told her. "Good, honest work. Nothing to turn your nose up at. It gets the money for the rent the same way anything else does. How much you think you're going to make as a nurse, anyway? Probably nowhere near as much as you can on a busy Friday night at the restaurant."

The problem lay in that not every night at the restaurant was a busy Friday night. And she couldn't budget her money beyond next month, much less through tomorrow because of it.

She found herself rubbing her belly and sighing. No matter what happened, she'd make sure her little girl trained for a good career. Got some college. Worked a job that didn't bleed the life out of you.

"Uh-oh. Don't look now, but that hunk of a man

you've been running around with lately just walked in the door."

Megan gaped at her. "I'm not running around with anyone."

Genie smiled at her. "It's not me you should be telling that." She poked her thumb over her shoulder.

Megan put her shoes on and went behind the counter to wash her hands in the sink there. When she turned back around, Eddie was sitting where she had been.

"Can I get you some lunch?" she asked.

Why was it every time he looked at her she felt like she was being sized up?

"No, thanks," he said. "I just stopped by to bring you these."

Megan squinted at the keys he laid on the counter and then pushed in her direction. They weren't her keys. She could tell by the black plastic holders on the top. And was that one of those electronic locking remotes?

"Those aren't mine."

Eddie grinned at her. "They are now."

Megan's heartbeat picked up in her chest. She edged around the counter.

"He bought you a car?" Genie whispered as she passed.

"Shh."

Megan didn't stop until she stood outside the restaurant door. She scanned the parking lot, but could barely make anything out in her shock. All she knew was that she didn't see the Crown Vic anywhere.

"Here." Eddie appeared beside her and handed her the keys she'd left on the counter.

She stood there staring at them in her hand for a long moment.

"Press the alarm button on the key bob."

"Alarm button?"

He held the small remote up and pointed to a button that showed the outline of a car in red. She pushed it.

Right in front of her the horn of a small, silver SUV began beeping.

Eddie reached for her hand and switched it back off as she stood staring in disbelief.

"It's not new or anything," Eddie said, pressing a button that unlocked the doors as he ushered her toward the driver's side. "But it's safe. And it's one of the hybrids, so not only is it yellow…no that's not it…what do they call it?"

"Green?"

"Yes. Not only is it green, it should save on gas." He shook his head. "I can only imagine what you were emptying into the tank of your old clunker."

"A lot."

He held open the door. "Climb in."

She hesitated. "Eddie…"

"What?"

"What did you do with my car?"

"This is your car now, Megan. I traded in the Crown Vic for it. All you have to do is stop by the dealership and sign the papers and it's yours."

She swallowed hard. What was this going to cost her?

Even as she thought it, she found herself caressing the leather seat inside. Her mother was going to freak.

Against her better judgment, she climbed in. Eddie showed her how to electronically adjust the seat and mirrors. She turned on the ignition, the sound of a country station playing "She Thinks My Tractor's Sexy" filling her ears and a blast of heat hitting her face.

Oh, it smelled so good.

The ding-ding of the open-door alert jerked her out of her temporary insanity.

She quickly climbed out of the car. "I can't afford this."

Eddie blinked at her and then reached in to switch off the engine. "What do you mean?"

Megan crossed her arms. "How much are the monthly payments, Eddie? I can't possibly afford this. I couldn't even afford to get my last car fixed."

"Your last car was beyond repair."

"Well, I'm just going to have to find a way to get it fixed."

She began stalking back toward the restaurant.

"Megan, you don't understand. This car...it's yours. Not after five years of payments. Flat out. Free and clear. There are no payments you have to make."

Megan's footsteps slowed. "What?" she whispered.

She slowly turned back to find him grinning at her. "I can't have the mother of my child driving a death trap now, can I?"

Megan was having trouble registering what he was saying.

He'd bought her a car?

It didn't make any sense.

"Here, catch." Eddie tossed her the keys. She just barely caught them. "Can you take a fifteen-minute break to give me a ride to pick up my truck? Then there are the papers you need to sign at the dealer. Maybe you should take a half hour...."

THE DAY WAS A COOL one, but Eddie had worked up a sweat painting the exterior of the house. He'd spent the day before scraping and applying primer. Where the color had been a dingy white before, he'd purposely chosen a warm peach now, with a darker green that reminded him of Megan's eyes for the trim.

During the daylight hours, he worked on the exterior, at night he saw to chores inside. He'd stripped the woodwork and sanded the old pine floors, refinished the cabinets and replaced some of the bathroom fixtures. He wanted to replace the tub, but that would have to wait. For now he'd scrubbed it down and spray painted it with epoxy. Even though it shone like new, it wasn't. And it would bother him until he replaced it.

He hadn't had a chance to get any furniture yet, but that was okay. He had plenty of time for that. For now, he wanted to get as much work in before he reported for his new construction job next week. Then when spring came around, he had another landscaping gig lined up for the weekends. The jobs combined should give him the money he needed.

He wiped his brow with the back of his wrist. His plan might not be going as he imagined, but he'd learned the hard way during his time in the Middle East that improvisation was everything. You had to think quick on your feet in order to stay alive.

He dipped the brush into the paint and tapped off the excess before seeing to the last upper quarter of this section. He'd have to move the ladder to the other side next.

The sound of a car pulling into the gravel drive pulled his attention there. A silver SUV.

Megan.

As it did every time he saw her, his chest drew tight. As did other areas of his anatomy that he was determined to ignore just now.

He watched her get out of the car in her waitress uniform and walk toward him. She held up what looked like an envelope. "Do you mind telling me the meaning of this?"

Eddie squinted at her. He couldn't imagine what had

gotten her so worked up. But he knew it couldn't be good for the baby.

He rested the brush against the top of the can and climbed down from the ladder.

He wiped his hands on his T-shirt before accepting the envelope from her. He frowned.

"It's a check."

She tsked. "I know it's a check. It's just that now that you're back, I thought you'd stop sending them."

"Why would I do that?"

She rubbed her face with her hand. She looked tired. And sexy as all get-out.

"Come on, why don't we go inside. I can fix you some herbal tea."

"Herbal tea…?" She bit her bottom lip then gestured toward the door. "Might as well. Because the talk you and I are about to have has been a long time coming…."

5

EDDIE WAS SITTING on one of the two kitchen chairs, hoping Megan would take his lead and sit in the other. Instead, she paced the floor, back and forth and back again. He watched her practical white shoes and tried not to let his gaze trail farther up to her perfectly shaped calves to the hem of her skirt and what he knew lay underneath.

"I don't get you," she was saying for the third time. "I mean, you not so much as blink when I tell you I'm pregnant…"

"I found out in a letter. Your letter."

"You know what I'm trying to say. Anyway, the next thing I know, you're out of the military and you're… well, you're…doing things for me…."

Her face contorted as she tried to make sense out of what she was saying. He sure hoped she succeeded, because she was making him dizzy with all that pacing. And her off-kilter logic wasn't helping any, either.

"The house…it's changed," she said, skipping to another subject.

He'd washed his face and hands when they'd come in and made her a cup of chamomile tea that he'd read somewhere was safe for her to drink, and now he picked up the kitchen towel from the table next to her un-touched cup and pretended to dry his hands.

"Yes," he said noncommittally.

There might be some things he couldn't help changing about his plan, but wherever he could keep it on track, he would.

"Nice. I like what you're doing. It'll be pretty once you're done."

He cleared his throat. "You were saying?"

"I was saying…"

Taking in the work he'd done seemed to calm her and she finally sat down opposite him and took a sip of the tea, murmuring a quiet thank-you.

"You're welcome."

She glared at him.

Whoa.

What had he done to get her all worked up?

"See, that's just it. Exactly what I'm talking about."

"What is?"

"Your doing things for me that I don't ask for. Or you don't ask me if I want." She sank into the chair. "You know what I mean."

"Actually, I don't." He held the towel in his hands as he leaned his forearms against his knees. "Why don't you trying explaining it to me in terms a five-year-old could understand."

She slowly sipped the tea, holding his gaze over the rim of the cup. He had the feeling this was going to be a long conversation.

MEGAN WAS TIED UP in knots. The part of her brain that wasn't muddled by emotion and hormones told her she should be thankful that Eddie wanted to be involved. Wasn't that what every mother hoped for? An involved father? For all intents and purposes it appeared Eddie was in this almost as much as she was.

Why, then, did she hurt?

With each check, every gift, she felt…dirty, somehow. As if Eddie felt she was looking for financial support.

Her heart wanted far more than that.

She sucked in a deep breath. "Tell me, Eddie, what are you looking for in all of this?"

He looked at her unblinkingly. "I want to do my duty."

She made a sound of frustration and got up to pace again.

"What? Since when is it a sin to do the right thing?"

"And who decides what that is? What duty means?"

He appeared confused.

Which was only fair, because she was confused. By him, by her pregnancy, by their situation.

"Look, Eddie, it's not that I don't appreciate what you've been doing…."

He waited patiently and then prompted, "But?"

"But…but…there's something not right about this entire situation. You're doing things without asking me."

"The car."

"It's not just the car, but yes, that's part of it." She fought to hold on to the train of thought before it ran through her fingers. "When we first spoke on the phone, after you received my letter, you didn't ask me if I needed money, or how much…you just started sending monthly checks."

He looked crestfallen. "It's not enough? God, I'm sorry, Megan. I never thought I should be giving more—"

She watched in shock as he got up and went to a kitchen drawer, taking out what looked like a checkbook.

"Eddie! You better not write me another check or I swear to God I won't be responsible for what I do next."

His hand tensed in midreach for a pen. She marched over and slid the checkbook from the counter and then slammed it back into the drawer.

"I don't get it," he said.

She picked up the check she'd received in the mail that day that lay on the table and held it up. "You don't have to send me the money. Not yet. Child support begins after the child is born."

She ripped the check in half.

"Don't do that, Megan. That money's as much for you as it is the baby."

"I don't want your money, Eddie."

She bit her bottom lip, realizing what she'd just said.

What did she want?

She felt ridiculously close to tears.

He came to stand in front of her, looking nearly as frustrated as she felt.

"Do you see the house around you, Megan? Go ahead. Take a good look."

She squinted at him rather than doing as he requested.

"Look at it!"

She did. If only because she had to glance away from him for fear that she would dissolve into tears.

She stepped closer to the bedrooms, immediately seeing the bed they'd spent that incredible night in. Then she spotted something else. Something in the next room.

It was a crib.

Her heart pitched to her feet and then back up again, sitting higher somehow than it had before.

"That's right. This place, this house…I'm fixing it up for you. For you and our child."

"What?" she whispered.

She turned and looked at him hopefully.

"I inherited it and the property when my mother died a couple of years ago. I own it, free and clear." He looked around. "I figured that since your mother and you live together, that you couldn't leave her hanging,

so I thought she could stay in the baby's room until he…
or she…is born, and by then I'll have added on another
room—a master with bath—and she could take the first
one."

He'd even thought of her mother?

The tears that had been threatening for a better part
of an hour tumbled over her lower lashes, burning her
cheeks as she looked at the blur of a man who was doing
so much for her without her having uttered a word.

She hadn't even known they made men like that anymore. Certainly, she'd never met one.

Until now.

She crossed the room and slid into his arms. He held
his hands aloft for a few moments and then wrapped
them around her, holding her close.

Slowly, her tears began to subside. She was amused
by the irony. She'd come here to beg him to stop giving
and he'd given her the ultimate gift: a home.

As she cleared the moisture from her cheeks with
her hand, the unmistakable scent of pure Eddie filled
her senses.

She rested her lips against his neck, telling herself she
just wanted one kiss. His skin tasted delectably salty and
one kiss led to two…then three. Then Eddie groaned
and sought to kiss her back.

He curved his hand under her chin and tilted her face
up, claiming her mouth tenderly.

She wanted to apologize for all that she'd said, for
marching in here and throwing everything into turmoil
for no good reason. But she suddenly couldn't seem to
catch her breath.

Before she could blink he had swept her up again and
carried her to his bedroom. She scooted back in order
to accommodate him, not protesting when he put on pro-

tection. She merely peeled off her own clothes and patiently waited for him to join her.

And join her he did....

Megan lost her breath entirely as he entered her in one long, slow stroke. She couldn't recall a time when she'd felt so connected to another human being. This man did things to her that no one before him had. He sensed what she needed before she even knew she wanted it.

For the first time she envisioned a future that she hadn't dared even dream of before. One of a family, a happy family, living together, loving together, laughing together. None of it had ever been a part of her life. She had never known her father. Had never come close to having a stepfather. It had always just been her and her mother, mostly struggling to make ends meet.

Now, she held Eddie's handsome face in her hands and kissed him deeply, passionately, tangling her tongue with his even as their hips melded together then parted.

She reached climax too soon again. But rather than move away as he'd tried to do the first time, he kissed her deeply and then made the moves necessary to roll her over until she was on all fours.

Heat, sure and swift, washed over Megan as she grasped the iron headboard tightly, bracing herself as he entered her from behind.

The moan that filled her ears was surely hers, but it was so foreign to her as to be unrecognizable. While hormones might be partially to credit for the climactic emotions swirling within her, she knew Eddie was mostly responsible. He filled her so completely, stroking her with a mastery that left her wondering if she'd ever be able to get enough of him or his lovemaking.

His strokes became faster, quicker, his fingers on her hips tightening as he held her still even as she strained to bear back. Up and up and up she flew with each slap of flesh against flesh. Her rapid breathing mingled with his…her cries as she reached a second, even more spectacular orgasm sounding with his groans….

AN HOUR LATER, Eddie held Megan close to his side, watching as the sun set outside the window. Somewhere a voice told him he should go out and cover the paint can he'd left open, take down the ladder before any neighborhood kids could get into trouble. But he could do nothing but lie there and count the beats of Megan's heart where her chest rested against the side of his.

He felt something move a little farther down. His eyes widened.

"Did you feel that?" he whispered, sliding his hand down between them until it rested against her stomach.

Megan rubbed her chin against his shoulder. "It's probably the baby," she said softly. "Then again, it could be gas."

He leaned back to look into her face and she laughed. "It's the baby."

He was floored as he followed the movements. Kicking? Tumbling? He was amazed to think that just a thin wall of flesh separated him from his child. A child that was growing bigger with each day and would soon be out, looking to him for protection and love.

"Do you think he's upset that we…" He trailed off. "That we're being so active?"

"She," Megan stressed, "doesn't have a clue what's going on. For all she knows, I've just had a busy night at the restaurant."

"You mean he…she moves around this much all the time?"

"Mmm."

She stroked the hair on his chest and then picked up his dog tags. She frowned as she read the name.

"Frances Drake Cash?"

His throat tightened. It had been a long, long time since he'd heard the name said aloud. "My father," he said. He picked up the other set of tags. "These are mine."

She looked up at him. "Do you always wear both sets?"

"Except on the battlefield. The captain thought it might be cause for confusion if…"

He heard the quiet click as she swallowed. "If you were KIA?"

He nodded as he wrapped his hand around both sets. "I never knew my dad. He died in combat before I was born."

The room was silent for a long time. Or so it seemed to Eddie as he remembered the somber quietness of his life as an only child to a single mother.

"Is that why you didn't sign up for another tour?" she asked.

He stared into her eyes.

He'd forgotten he'd told her he intended to go career when they'd met six months before.

"Yes," he said simply. "I couldn't bear it if something happened to me and I couldn't…I couldn't be a father to this child."

He caressed her bare back and then pulled the blankets up to cover her in case she was cold.

"Are you hungry?" he asked. "I can go make us some sandwiches."

"I'm fine." She smiled, her hair a tousled halo around her sexy head. "You're at risk of spoiling me, you know?" She cuddled closer and closed her eyes. "I could definitely get used to this."

Eddie rested his chin on top of her head.

"I figure that I should be done with the house in a week. You and your mom can start moving in then, if you like."

She kissed his shoulder. "Sounds nice."

"I've already found a room in the old Virginian Hotel downtown. Just let me know when you plan to move in and I'll be out...."

For days, Eddie wouldn't have a clue what he'd said or done wrong. All he knew was that he'd never seen a woman—never mind a pregnant one—move so far so fast as when Megan got up from the bed and stalked from the house without a single word.

And he never wanted to again.

6

MEGAN FELT MELANCHOLIA that she couldn't exactly pinpoint the cause of, but that mowed the grass from under her nonetheless.

Her mother watched her for four full days before finally commenting. Megan supposed she should be grateful Becky Sue had given her that long. But she instead wished she could have waited a little longer.

"I'm going to say this one thing and then I'll shut up again," her mother said from behind the coupon section of the Sunday paper. They'd had a light breakfast of toast and oatmeal at the two-chair table in the kitchen, trading sections of the newspaper. Megan was pretending the Living section did it for her when honestly she couldn't seem to finish a sentence and had to go back and read it again.

She stiffened at her mother's words, but didn't indicate in any other way that she'd heard her.

"Girl, don't you think you're setting the bar a little high here?"

Megan slapped the paper down. "What?"

Her mother peered at her over a coupon for coffee. "The guy buys you a car, sends you a monthly check, takes care of you better than any husband that I'm familiar with, and yet you're determined to chase him away, like he's committed some horrible crime only you seem to be aware of and aren't sharing with anyone else."

"Maybe it's because he has."

Becky Sue sighed and mumbled under her breath, "Yes, well, if he has, I've seen no evidence of it."

"Well, excuse me for thinking you should be more concerned with my well-being here than his."

Her mother put the coupons down altogether. "Ah, yes. I think we've hit on the heart of the problem here, haven't we?"

Megan narrowed her eyes. "What?"

"For the past two weeks all I've been hearing about is you, you, you. How you feel about this, how Eddie made you feel about that. Now I know that some of it's those awful hormones running amok, but God, girl, I can't count the times I had to stop myself from smacking you up upside the head with the closest available object."

Megan knew she was speaking figuratively, but she couldn't help gaping at her mother anyway.

Becky Sue seemed to realize that she wasn't getting anywhere and sighed again. "Look, Megan, all I'm trying to say is that this isn't about you anymore. It's about that baby you're carrying. It's about my grandchild. Your child. Eddie's child. And you're going to have to stop thinking in terms having to do with only you and deal with what's the best for him or her."

"Like you did with me?"

Her mother blanched.

"I'm sorry. That was uncalled for."

"No matter what, Megan, I always tried my best with you. And I always put you first. Like that transfer offer to Boston that you didn't want me to take because you were a year into high school and didn't want to lose your friends. Like when you met Joss, one of the few men I ever dated, and told me you didn't like him, so I dumped him the next day. If there was a dollar extra to be had, it went for something for you. School supplies, a hair ribbon, a pair of socks, you always came first."

She reached across the table and took Megan's hands in hers.

"And you still do."

Megan blinked back tears.

Becky Sue pulled her hands back and returned to her coupon hunting. "At least until that grandchild of mine comes into the world." She gave her a warning glance. "Then, all bets are off."

Megan got up to clear the plates, feeling like she had been hit with everything within her mother's reach.

THIS HAD TO HAVE been the longest week of his life, up to and including his first tour patrolling Fallujah, one of the most violent areas of Iraq in the beginning of the war.

Eddie finished work on the house, began his job with the construction company for which he'd worked before enlisting, and essentially beat his head against the wall trying to figure out what he'd done wrong.

Stubborn woman. Megan wouldn't even take his calls. And when he'd scraped up the courage to go to the restaurant, she'd done everything she could to avoid him. Successfully, because he wasn't about to make a scene…and he was pretty sure she knew that.

Which left him…where?

It was a Sunday morning and he'd shown up at the construction work site for a couple hours, picking up a bag of groceries on his way home.

Home. Now there was a word. He'd strived hard to make the house a place Megan would be pleased to call home. It didn't resemble anything he was used to growing up. Oh, the dimensions were the same, but everything else had changed. It even smelled different.

He put cartons of juice and milk in the refrigerator and stocked the cabinet with cans of soup and a box of crackers.

He tucked the bag into the recycling bin and then leaned against the counter with his arms crossed, unsure what he should do next. There was the yard, but he'd planned to wait until spring before doing any major landscaping. There was very little furniture because he'd thought Megan would want to see to most of that herself.

Megan…

It seemed that the name had been front and center in his mind ever since he'd learned she was pregnant. He frowned. Actually, that wasn't true. She'd monopolized his thoughts since the first moment he'd laid eyes on her. She'd mesmerized him with her wit, her warm smile and her sexy, uninhibited ways. She'd seemed to crawl under his very skin and it was there she'd remained.

The baby was important, yes. But the woman herself was even more important to him.

The thought of being a father filled him with fear and pride and love. But the thought of being a noncustodial parent scared the shit out of him. Forget that he wouldn't have a major impact on the kid's life, wouldn't be there for his or her first words, first steps, first day of kindergarten.

The thought of having to see Megan and not be able to touch her when he picked up the child or dropped him or her off absolutely floored him.

The telephone at his elbow rang. Only three people had the number. Megan. Base personnel. And Marine Lieutenant Matt Guerrero so he could keep up with what was happening in the court-martial hanging over Captain Brian Justice's head for a crime he didn't commit.

He hoped the caller was the first on his list.

He picked up in the middle of the second ring. "Hello?"

"Eddie?"

Megan…

MEGAN COULDN'T SEEM to stop straightening up the apartment. She'd fluffed the sofa cushions no fewer than three times, wiped the kitchen counter twice, and thought about getting out the vacuum for another once-over. If she'd thought it would help the old, green shag carpeting, she would have. But at this point, nothing was going to improve on that.

It was either tidy up or obsess over her appearance in the bathroom mirror. But since it didn't appear Eddie was interested in her beyond some great sex and the child they were expecting…well, nothing she did would help in that area, either, now, would it?

Megan slowed her movements as she took the sandwiches she'd made earlier out of the refrigerator and arranged them on a plate. Her mother was right. She owed the baby growing within her every consideration, no matter how much it hurt her personally. She couldn't exactly pinpoint when she'd come to want something else from Eddie. Perhaps it was because she'd never had to direct her energy or thoughts at getting him to support their child or plan to take an active role in his or her life that had opened up possibilities for more.

More specifically, the whole nine yards. Marriage. Children. A house with a white picket fence.

She finished with the plate and washed her hands again, following with a liberal application of lotion that she automatically also applied to the stretching skin of her belly.

There was a knock at the front door. She started, as if she hadn't spent the past hour waiting for Eddie to arrive. She quickly readjusted her sweater, tucked her hair behind her ears and took the two steps necessary to open the door.

Damn, but he looked good. As usual. He wore a pair of jeans and a soft dark blue cotton shirt buttoned over a T-shirt. His hair was damp and she could only guess that he'd just gotten out of the shower. Something a quick intake of breath verified as the smell of his soap filled her nose.

He looked good enough to eat with a spoon. Good thing she'd fixed a lunch that could be eaten without utensils.

"Come in," she said quietly.

He hesitated, and then stepped around her. His presence alone seemed to make the apartment feel that much smaller. He couldn't move without bumping one of the tree trunks he called legs against some piece of secondhand furniture.

Megan smiled. "Please, have a seat anywhere you like," she said. "I'll just be a minute."

He surprised her by grasping her arm. "Can we wait...for lunch?" he asked, his expression earnest. "I don't think I could eat anything anyway. Not before hearing what you have to say."

She swallowed thickly. He seemed in as bad mental shape as she felt.

"Sure," she said, but stopped short of admitting that she wouldn't have been able to eat, either. Of course, inviting him over for lunch had been the polite thing to do. It had sounded better than "get over here, we need to talk."

She led the way toward the couch and sat, slightly disappointed when he chose a chair next to her rather than the spot on the couch she'd purposely left open.

If she'd needed any more proof that he wasn't interested in her, she'd just gotten it.

She cleared her throat, realizing that he was waiting for her to say her piece.

"First, um, I guess I should say that I'm sorry...." she began, although she was afraid she wouldn't be able to say the words at all.

He waited, as if expecting more. Then said, "Sorry for what?"

She squinted at him. "Sorry for behaving the way I did the other night."

"Oh. That."

What else would she be talking about?

God, had she known this was going to be so difficult, she would never have attempted it.

Her hand automatically went to her stomach. She rested it there, a reminder of why she was doing this.

"Second...I want to thank you." The words stuck in her throat. Not because they weren't true, but because they were. "You've been so...thoughtful when it comes to the baby." She smiled as she looked at her stomach. "This baby is going to have a good life."

Silence reigned for a few moments. Then Eddie said, "But..."

Megan sucked her bottom lip between her teeth. No matter how much she wanted to tell him of her hopes, her dreams, that's not what she'd invited him over for.

She shook her head. "There are no buts."

His warm grin caught her off guard. "There are always a few buts."

But I'd give everything up...the car, the house, the checks, if only you'd love me, her heart whispered.

She looked down again, willing herself not to say anything.

"Look, Megan, I know I could have handled all of this better...."

"Couldn't we all?"

"I just want you to know that I never meant to sleep with you."

His words stung her heart like a thousand bees.

"Truth is," he continued, unaware of her reaction, "I've been working out this plan ever since I learned the news that, um, we were expecting."

His use of the pronoun made her smile despite her bone-deep sadness.

"And ever since I've gotten back, time and time again, those plans have suffered setbacks, hit speed bumps and ultimately have been derailed altogether."

Megan laughed without humor. "Tell me about it. My life hasn't been exactly going according to plan, either."

Silence again. Megan could make out the sound of the neighbors in the next apartment arguing.

"I know it's probably none of my business, but where...where are you getting all this money?" she asked.

"I'm not rich, if that's what you mean." He shifted in the chair. "When I first went into the service, I sent my checks home to my mother every month. I'd expected for her to use them. Instead she deposited them. Then when she passed away a couple of years ago, I inherited the house along with a small life insurance policy." He cleared his throat. "Like I said, it's not much.

But it's allowing me to do what I can for you and our child."

"What about what you want, Eddie? You should be doing what you want. It's your money. You worked for it. What do you want to do?"

His gaze captured hers. "I'm doing exactly what I want to do."

"Because of the baby."

He blinked, surprised. "No, Megan, because of you."

Her heart gave a little lurch.

Eddie looked down at where he'd clasped his hands between his knees. Such strong hands capable of great gentleness. She watched as he shook his head, and when he looked up, he was smiling.

"God, I'm so stupid," he said.

"What?"

"I was so determined on going through my plans step-by-step that I never stopped to consider that the new developments had disrupted them entirely."

"I'm not sure I'm following you." But, oh, she did. She wanted to follow him everywhere.

"Megan, all this I'm doing…it's not just for the baby. It's for you. It's for us."

"But you said you were going to move into the downtown hotel."

He appeared to be trying to work out the best way to say something.

"Fine. This probably isn't going to be pretty. And nowhere in sight is a bottle of fine wine or an expensive steak dinner and soft music, but…"

She watched as he worked the ring on his right ring finger free. His marine insignia ring. Then he got up and dropped to one knee in front of her.

At just that moment, the front door opened and in breezed her mother.

Megan gasped. "Mother, go!"

"Well, damn me to hell and back for interrupting. In case you've forgotten, missy, I live here, too."

"It's all right," Eddie said. "She can stay."

Megan motioned for him to continue, terrified he might change his mind.

"At every turn, you've shot down my advances, Megan. I bought you a car, you tried to return it. I sent you a check, you ripped it up. I fixed up a house for you, and you stormed out as if I'd given you a leaky tent." He cleared his throat. "I'd worked out a plan that went step-by-step. What I hadn't factored in was how you might be feeling." He searched her eyes. "You thought I was doing all of this only because of the baby, didn't you?"

Megan was aware of her mother taking a dining-room chair and turning it so she could watch them from a position of comfort.

"Well, then, move in with me because I love you."

She was incapable of speech.

"Marry me, because I love you."

He wouldn't…couldn't stoop to pretending something he didn't feel out of his skewed sense of honor. Would he?

"You don't even know me," she whispered.

"I know how I feel about you," he said. "And I now think I know how you feel about me."

"Why were you going to move into the hotel then?" she whispered.

"Because I thought that's what you'd want until we got married."

Megan couldn't have thrown herself more forcefully into Eddie's arms, nearly knocking him over. She kissed him and kissed him and kissed him again.

He chuckled and held her face, kissing her back.

"I suppose I should have known from the moment I read your letter that life never goes according to plan," he said. "But now I'm left without the diamond ring I wanted to buy you. But I'd be honored if you'd accept this in lieu of the ring you pick out."

He slid his marine ring onto her finger and they both stared at it, smiling.

"Oh, Lord. You both are the silliest things I've seen since those damn plastic birds that tip back and forth on their own."

Eddie kissed Megan again and then forced himself to let her go as he got to his feet.

"I'm sorry, Mrs. Walker. I'd wanted to ask your permission first...."

She waved him away, trying for irritated, but Megan could tell by the color on her cheeks that she was as charmed as she was. "I don't hold her ownership papers."

"Yes, but we'd like to have you move in with our family at the house."

Becky Sue gaped at him. "Are you nuts? Given the way the two of you probably go at it, I'd never get a night's rest." She crossed her arms. "As luck would have it, I happen to have one or two backup plans of my own."

Megan laughed as she put her arms around Eddie's waist. He rested his hand on her belly even as he cupped her behind well out of her mother's eyeshot.

"What say we go home?" she said.

"Now that's exactly what I had planned...."

Mateo

1

THIS WASN'T THE coming home on a month's leave he would have imagined.

Matt Guerrero remembered times when there were flags waving and tears falling at the Rickenbacker Air National Guard Base just outside Columbus, Ohio, his three kids scrambling to be the first to be picked up, and his wife, Ana, hugging him as if her very life depended on it, her lush body reminding him of everything that was home.

Now two of his kids were teenagers, the youngest, Teresa, a full-blown tween, all surely too "grown" for such sappy events, and his wife…

"This the place, buddy?"

Matt turned to face the taxi driver, almost having forgotten where he was. "Um, yes. Thanks, man."

He paid the fare and got out of the car, hauling his duffel to sit on the curb beside him.

Home.

The two-story house before him that he'd lived in for almost two decades once might have held a crayon-drawn banner saying, "Welcome Home." There would have been punch and cake and hard hugs as family came together to help him reintegrate into civilian life for the short time he was home.

Of course, all of that was over a decade go, during

his first six-year military tour. He'd "retired" from the Corps and gone to college, taking a double course load in order to get his technical engineering degree in half the time. He'd gone on to start a company, G&S Consulting, with Ana's brother Pedro, and which now employed more than fifty full-time and another twenty-five part-time workers, a good percentage of whom were college interns who would go on to become full-time once they graduated.

He'd remained a marine reservist for no specific reason other than that's what ex-marines did, reporting for training one weekend a month and two weeks every summer, having no idea that he'd be called back into service four years ago at age thirty-four.

A neighborhood dog barked, jarring him from his reverie.

He hauled his bag up and stepped up the front walk in his standard-issue fatigues, feeling oddly out of place in the middle-class neighborhood after spending the past fourteen months patrolling the hot, gritty streets of Baghdad. It was January in the Columbus suburbs, a month after the holidays, but Christmas lights were still up. He found his house keys, but ended up not needing them as the door opened easily inward.

"I'm home," he called out.

He heard nothing but the sound of rap music from upstairs.

He dropped his bag near the foot of the stairs and reconnoitered the first floor, finding dirty dishes in the sink, no sign of dinner. He backtracked and grabbed his bag again and went upstairs. No one in the master bedroom where he left his duffel on the bed, or in the master bath or the main bath. He tried to push open his sixteen-year-old son Johnny's door, but it was locked, a

Keep Out sign posted on the outside. The next room belonged to his youngest daughter, Teresa—the Pepto-Bismol pink-on-pink color scheme made him smile and itch at the same time. The next room used to look just as frilly, but he noticed through the slightly open door that posters of teenage singing stars and American Idols now covered the worst of it. This one belonged to his oldest, seventeen-year-old Lola. He pushed the door inward to find her lying lengthwise across her bed, swaying her feet in the air as she talked on her cell phone.

Damn, but this had to be the hardest part of coming home. Seeing how much everyone had changed while he'd been away. While he wasn't looking, Lola had turned into a beautiful woman.

But she was still his daughter.

He reached out and grabbed her ankle.

He took some enjoyment in her squeak of fear as she rolled over and tried to extricate her foot.

"Daddy!"

Now that was a sound capable of undoing any man.

He welcomed the buck-ten of his flesh and blood into his arms and squeezed tight, reminded for a moment of those times at the airfield.

"What are you doing here? We weren't expecting you until Friday."

"I know. I got in early," he said. And he hadn't told Ana of the change in plans for reasons he had yet to completely uncover. He had called, but when he'd been sent to her voice mail, he'd merely said, "I'm looking forward to seeing you," and didn't say anything about coming home early.

"You left the front door unlocked. I could have been a burglar looking to expand my felony crimes to rape."

She made a face. "I didn't leave it unlocked. Johnny must have when he left about an hour ago."

The door had been unlocked for an hour. He would never have tolerated that before. And he didn't have a big threshold for tolerance now, either. Ana sometimes complained that he ran the house like a military camp. He argued that he was just keeping them all safe.

Lola told whomever she was talking to that she'd call back and then turned down the music.

"Where is everyone?" he asked.

"Teresa is over at her friend Rebecca's until tomorrow, Johnny's at the mall with his friends and Mom's at the studio." She looked stricken. "I can't believe you came home and nobody knew anything. Mom's got that party planned and everything."

Her words cheered him, but not by much. He'd purposely come home to see how day-to-day life was proceeding in the Guerrero household beyond what would have been the honeymoon stage of his official return.

"What do you mean your mom's at the studio? She getting her hair done?"

"No, silly." She sat down next to him. Or, rather, more like bounced. "She's at the dance studio. She's teaching."

Ana was working? Why would Ana need to work? He knew Pedro was supplying her with a monthly dividend check. And then there was his military pay.

Fear struck him. Had something happened that she hadn't told him?

"What's the name of the studio?" he asked.

Lola considered him warily, reminding him a little too much of her mother. Both of them had always seemed uncannily capable of reading his intentions. And right now his intention was to get to the bottom of what was going on.

Five minutes later, he was calling up to his daughter from the front door.

"Where in the hell is my car?"

Lola's hair created a shifting curtain where she leaned over to meet his gaze from the upstairs hall. "Johnny took it. Use his. The keys are in the basket on the hall table."

Matt stood in the driveway, staring at the pile of junk that had been traded for his five-year-old Highlander.

"No way," he muttered under his breath. "No effin' way."

He climbed into the twenty-year-old Mazda with rust holes the size of his clenched fists and coughed as the oil-deprived engine started with a deafening pop.

HE WOULD BE HOME in three days.

Ana Diaz Guerrero swallowed the butterflies trying to escape her stomach and continued stretching at the dance bar, repositioning her feet and bending deeply, ignoring her reflection in the mirror behind it. One of the most difficult things about being a marine wife was the waiting. Forever the waiting. And the days leading up to scheduled leave were the hardest, every second ticking by like an hour.

She couldn't remember a time in her adult life when Mateo Guerrero wasn't the center of her universe. The tall, gruff-talking hunk with the broad shoulders and even broader grin. He'd proposed to her on their third date at McDonald's. At first she'd been so surprised, she hadn't known what to say. Then she'd thrown herself headlong into his arms, knocking their dinner tray off the table, sending french fries flying.

She'd never regretted one moment of her life with him. She'd loved him and he'd loved her back.

And the sex…

She shivered just thinking of what the man was capable of in bed. He swam oceans and moved mountains in order to bring her multiple orgasms, putting the same kind of attention that had gone into making him a marine into bringing her joy.

And, oh, what joy he'd brought her. As their three kids were walking testament to.

Dolores aka Lola was born exactly nine months to the day of their wedding. Johnny was born nine months to the day after Matt's first home leave during his first tour of duty where he'd been stationed in Bosnia. And little Teresa had been born exactly nine months after he'd finally been given an honorable discharge and embraced civilian life with the same passion with which he'd embraced the military.

Ana took a deep breath, disappointed at the tears burning her eyes. They'd gone through so very much during those years. And then had moved on to form a life and family together of which her friends were envious.

But this time…this time was different. He'd left the service behind well over a decade earlier. It wasn't fair that she should have to sacrifice again. That her family should.

Of course, she still wasn't sure what bothered her more: that he was called back to service, or that he'd gone willingly and without objection, choosing the war over their family, their marriage.

Okay, if she didn't stop this, she was going to cry. Which was ridiculous really because arguably she shouldn't have any more tears left to shed.

Then there was that other ache that refused to go away…

She hadn't seen her husband, her Mateo, for fourteen long months. More than a year. Had missed two Christmases with him. Two New Year's Eves. And her heart hurt in a way that she could neither ignore nor withstand. She felt that she might go insane if she didn't kiss his lips, cradle him between her thighs.

But she couldn't do this again. Not anymore. If he continued to serve, she couldn't continue to make him the center of her universe. Because to do so would be to court complete disaster if something ever happened to him.

Her gaze drifted to the clock on the wall above the mirrors again. Only two minutes had passed. An entire lifetime before she could restart her life....

CHA-CHA'S DANCE Studio was in the OSU Gateway district of Columbus on North High Street, and despite it being midweek, Matt had a difficult time finding a parking spot. He hadn't changed before leaving the house and still wore his fatigues, his boots shined to a dark gloss. A few people he passed as he walked greeted him, thanking him for his service, and he acknowledged them on autopilot. He was too busy trying to figure out why his wife was working at a dance studio and how he was going to get in there without making a scene.

He soon found out he didn't have to worry about the second concern. The front window was apparently part of the main studio, a mirror that stretched the length of the opposite wall giving the room a much larger feel. And the window he was looking in must have been specially treated because in the reflection it looked like another mirror. Which probably meant that while passersby could look in, the dancers couldn't see out.

But Matt barely registered the polished wood floor, or the chairs along the side walls. His gaze immediately homed in on the woman at the bar in front of the opposite mirror.

Ana?

Matt felt as if a gust of cold air had robbed him of breath and any ability he had to breathe.

The woman had her back to him. Her silky black hair was longer than Ana's. She was slimmer than Ana. And she was wearing a type of close-fitting dress than Ana hadn't worn in years. But Mateo Castro Guerrero would know his Ana anywhere.

Over the years they'd evolved into older versions of themselves. His crow's-feet had grown deeper, his physique stockier. And Ana had grown more lush and fuller, had cut her hair shorter to reflect a lifestyle devoted more to raising her children than seducing a husband who was already madly in love with her.

But now…

It wasn't that far of a stretch to compare this Ana to the one he'd met so long ago. The one he'd proposed to over Big Macs and chocolate shakes. The one he could spend the entire night making love to no matter how early he had to get up in the morning.

The image combined with her increasing emotional distance from him during phone calls and e-mails over the past year created a knot in his gut that would be strong enough to anchor an aircraft carrier.

Ana moved. She was stretching her arm over, creating a long, arching line that enhanced her new, slimmer frame. Her legs seemed to go on forever, the heeled shoes giving her more height. She was a competitive dancer when they'd met, but she'd stopped shortly thereafter when she'd become pregnant with Lola. She used to display her trophies in their bedroom, but must have put them away a long time ago because he couldn't recall seeing them for years.

Matt tried to force himself to move toward the door, but his feet were cemented to the sidewalk. What would he say to her? What would she say to him? His mouth was dry of saliva and words.

Inside the studio, a door opened and a man entered. Matt's gaze moved to him as if in slo-mo. The man was maybe ten years younger than he was and wore black dance pants and a white shirt, and was smooth and suave where Matt was rough-and-tumble.

Ana turned and for a moment Matt thought she saw him, despite the treated window. She wore a faraway expression, an expectant one, as if she'd known he was coming home early and was even now waiting for him.

Then the man approached her and she looked caught off guard, but instantly recovered with a smile. He kissed her on both cheeks, went and pressed a button on a stereo and then took her hand to lead her in a dance.

Matt recognized an emotion not because it was one with which he was familiar, but because it so wholly consumed him, it seemed to burn his veins from the inside out.

He didn't have to be of Cuban heritage to know that the dance they were doing was the rumba, but it didn't hurt.

He also didn't have to be a marine to know that he was a breath away from a murderous rage.

His feet escaped the cement they'd been encased in a few minutes before and Matt marched toward the door, determined to defend his property....

2

FIFTEEN MINUTES LATER, Ana stood across the hood of her car from her husband, her heart beating a million miles a minute.

He was home, a small voice whispered.

He was home and he hadn't told her he was coming.

"I can't believe you did that," she said, her voice louder than she would have liked. "You should feel lucky that Lev didn't call the police. You could be charged with assault."

"Lev should feel lucky that I didn't knock him into the middle of next week."

"Oh, that's nice."

Ana had never seen Matt act the way he had in the studio. It had taken her a full minute to realize that the man in fatigues was actually her husband. One minute she'd been doing a rumba turn, the next a green blur had cut across the dance floor and jerked Lev from their dance hold and socked him right in the eye.

She'd instantly put herself between the two men, confronting her husband with shock. "Mateo!"

Thankfully Lev had held up his hand, saying no apology was necessary, although one clearly was. Then he'd excused himself to go get ice to put on his eye, which was sure to be black-and-blue in the morning.

Ana had gathered her things and left the studio, Matt following on her heels.

"Who in the hell is that, Ana?" he asked, his voice dangerously low.

There had always been something powerful about Matt. Something almost dangerous that had drawn her to him. He'd been a marine straight out of training when they'd met, and she'd been in awe of his strength and handsomeness. While she'd never given him anything to be jealous of, she'd always known he was capable. Had caught warning glances when at parties he thought her conversations with men went too long, or was aware of his often possessive public displays of affection, as if he were letting everyone else in the room know that she was his girl and he would do anything to keep it that way.

It had made her feel special. Loved.

Now she wanted to crawl into a hole and cry.

"Who do you think he is, Matt? He's my dance partner, for God's sake. We're training for a competition later this month."

"Competition? Lola told me that you're teaching."

"I am. But I also decided I wanted to compete again. Remember that I used to dance? Before I had Lola, and then Johnny? Before we settled into a routine that made me forget that I enjoyed dancing?"

So long ago that she'd even forgotten to hear the music. Deep drumbeats that she'd grown up with, that had shaped so much of her Cuban-American upbringing. She'd taken the kids to a family wedding last summer and the reception had featured a Cuban band. Where she might have ignored it, especially since her husband was halfway across the world putting his life at risk, instead she'd enjoyed a mojito and accepted a dance with one of her older cousins. The music had thread its way through her veins as surely as the alcohol and she'd known then that she'd found something to keep her busy. Something that made her feel like a woman again. A human being with human needs. And one of them was to feel alive. And if she couldn't do that with her husband, she could do it with dancing.

The expression on Matt's face tugged on her heart-strings. "Routine? Is that how you describe our marriage, Ana?"

She looked down, her voice barely above a whisper as she said, "No, that's how I describe our life, Matt. It became so routine that the moment you were called back to active duty, you jumped on the first transport out."

She took her keys from her purse and unlocked the door to her compact SUV, sliding behind the wheel. He tried opening the passenger door. She rolled down that window a couple of inches.

"Where's your car?" she asked.

"I drove Johnny's POS here because he has mine. He can come pick the damn thing up tomorrow. Let me in."

"Not on your life," she said and put the car into Reverse.

HIS FIRST NIGHT back and he was sleeping on the couch.

Matt lay in the dark of the family room, incapable of believing that Ana had locked herself in their bedroom, opening the door only to shove a pillow and blanket into his arms before slamming it shut again. She'd shouted that he needed to cool down. He'd told her that she needed to start acting like his wife.

It had taken seeing Lola staring at him from her bedroom doorway like a frightened deer to remind him that they weren't alone and that he needed to get control of himself.

Damn. How in the hell had he allowed things to spiral so quickly out of control? He'd come home to fix his marriage, not shatter it beyond repair. It's just that when he saw his wife in another man's arms, no matter how innocent she claimed it to be, he transformed into someone he recognized only in battle zones. A man determined to keep what was his—in the case of war, his life—at any cost.

But he wasn't in a war zone and Ana wasn't a piece of land to be claimed and protected. She was a woman who had proven herself at least as strong as the men he served with, if not stronger. For the first six years of their marriage, she had held their family together through thick and thin, seeing the kids through illnesses and difficulties even as she'd taken care of him.

He heard the garage door open and close and the nearby door open. His son, he had no doubt.

"Where have you been?" he broke the dead silence.

"Who's…Dad? Is that you?"

Matt lifted up onto an elbow and reached to switch on the lamp on the table behind him. He squinted at his sixteen-year-old son. Christ, where was the lanky teen he remembered? The one that complained he was smaller than the other guys at school? The skinny one with the concave chest who weight-trained and drank protein shakes in an effort to bulk up to no avail? He must have grown at least six inches since the last time Matt saw him, and put on at least thirty pounds.

"Answer my question first," Matt said, trying to hide his pride that his son was turning into such a powerful man.

"I…um…I was at the mall."

"Which closed at least two hours ago."

"My curfew isn't until midnight. It's ten till."

"But that doesn't explain why you were driving my car instead of your own."

"Oh."

Matt grinned inwardly at the kid's obvious chagrin. He stripped off the blanket and got up, hauling the teen into a bear hug.

"Christ, you're almost as big as me."

His son's body relaxed against his. "Impossible. Nobody's as big as you."

He pounded Johnny on the back and then stepped back and held his hand out palm up. His son automatically dropped his car keys into it.

"You filled it with gas?"

"I filled it with gas."

Matt grinned. "Good. Now let's go grab a sandwich while you tell me about everything that's been going on here for the past year...."

ANA WOKE UP IN the middle of the night hot and bothered, her breathing labored, her thighs squeezed tightly together. It was a familiar occurrence when Mateo was on active duty, but something she wasn't used to when he was home. Because when he was home she had access to him.

Usually.

She swallowed hard and pulled one of the decorative pillows from the empty side of the bed and placed it between her legs. But her body wasn't having any of it. It knew that the path to salvation lay just a staircase away.

No. She couldn't give in. Wouldn't give in. Matt had to learn that she was no longer that young girl happy to have whatever scraps of affection he had to throw her way.

She flinched, knowing that was unfair. Whenever he'd been with her during that first tour, and even during his last leave, he'd given her one hundred and ten percent. The problem lay in the lonely stretches in between. And the fact that even though the Internet and cell phones made communication easier than it had been even a decade ago, there was a big difference between right there and seeming to be right there.

The throbbing in her nether regions refused to go away. If anything, she seemed to grow more acutely aware of the clamoring for release. She'd usually see to the job herself with reminiscing about previous sack sessions with her husband and stroking fingers, but she refused to do it while he was home. It wasn't right.

She pulled the pillow out and rolled over to lie flat on her back, staring up at the ceiling, wide-eyed and wanting.

She thought she heard a sound outside the door. She lifted up on her shoulders and held her breath, listening. Matt? She'd unlocked the door before going to bed, a part of herself hoping that he would join her at some point during the night. Was he doing so now?

She got up and crept toward the door. Hearing nothing, she cracked it open to find the hall empty.

Her disappointment was complete.

Oh, the hell with it. Lord knew she'd done more wanton things in the past. And while her emotional argument with her husband was far from over, the fact that he was her husband, and she wanted him, currently took precedence over everything else.

Making sure the kids' doors were closed, she crept quietly down the steps and into the family room. She made out his form on the leather sectional sofa and heard his even breathing.

Shit. She really shouldn't do this. By surrendering to

her physical need of him, she would be surrendering much, much more.

"Ana?"

His voice reached out for her. Then he did, throwing back the blanket and stretching out a hand.

And, forgive her, she went straight to him without a second thought.

MAKING LOVE TO HIS wife wasn't just an experience, it was an event. Time seemed to slow, the world stopped turning, and all Matt could hear was the thick flow of blood through his veins, his total need for the woman in his arms humbling in its scale.

He expected her to say something in advance, indicate that their argument wasn't over, but she merely kissed him, openmouthed and hungry, displaying every ounce of longing he felt and more. A year and a half was a long time to be away from a woman you loved more than anything else on earth squared.

God, how could he have forgotten how she smelled? Like spicy gardenias. Her skin was smooth, her hair a soft cascading waterfall in his fingers. He tried to inhale her with his kiss, their rushed breathing loud in his ears. He went to turn her over on the couch, but she stayed him with her hands on his shoulders.

Matt's chest tightened as he watched her reach under her cotton nightgown and strip off her underwear, then take off the nightgown itself. Her breasts were high and rose tipped, her dark skin shimmering in the moonlight streaming through the balcony doors.

Hell, but she was even more beautiful than he remembered.

He reached up and caught her nipples against his rough palms, relishing her instant shiver as she swung her hair back and stretched her neck as if unable to believe his touch elicited such sensation. She restlessly licked her lips then bent and kissed him again even as she reached between them to free him from his drawstring pajamas. Within moments she held his hard length in her small hands. It didn't matter if it had been a day or a year since they'd been together, her complete rapture in touching him fascinated him. She'd once proclaimed that while she loved and was in love with him, she was in complete lust with his penis. Had even named it Pepe.

He watched as she slid down the length of his legs and took him into her mouth. His hips instantly bucked upward and she smiled, clearly enjoying the power she held over him. She licked and sucked as if he was a long-desired lollipop and she was after the sweet stuff that awaited in the middle.

He grasped her shoulders to hold her aloft when he was near climax. When he came, he wanted it to be with her....

3

ANA COULDN'T REMEMBER feeling so hot, so needy. She wiggled until she straddled Matt's hips. Okay, maybe that wasn't true. She always felt like she was a thrust away from self-combustion when she made love to her husband. If asked, she couldn't have explained exactly why. It was everything. It was nothing. Sometimes she felt as if it was because they were two halves of one person and that it was only when they were connected that she felt whole. Other times she thought that maybe it was because he answered to some unnamed want within her.

But to limit their incredible lovemaking to the purely physical was to say the sky was blue, but not mention the sea. Matt and she had come through so much together. From the instant they'd met, they'd never had eyes for another. Not once had she doubted this. And despite her anger earlier, it hurt to think that he thought her capable of betraying him with her heart, much less her body.

He was her life, her love, forever. She'd once believed that with everything that she was. And she longed to believe in that again.

She was so hot for him that she didn't need foreplay. She merely grasped his hard length and slid down over him to the hilt, her juices gushing out to cover his hot shaft.

Oh, yes…

Pure electricity ran over and under skin, making her feel shimmeringly, magnificently alive from her fingernails to her toes. He filled her to overflowing, his hot flesh melding with hers.

She brought her hips forward and then back again, her heart seeming to give a little jump with every move. He grasped her right breast as if marveling at the curved flesh, pinching her nipple, creating an electric arc between the sensitive tip and her womb. She reached back to grasp his legs to steady herself and to give him full access to her breasts, the position forcing him deeper.

He slid his hands from her breasts to her hips, moving his thumbs inward until they met at the apex of her thighs. Ana licked her lips restlessly, quickening the pace of her rocking, racing toward climax yet trying to hold back, yearning to prolong the golden sensations rippling through her.

Too late. Wave upon wave of the ultimate sweet surrender crashed over her. She grasped his shoulders, riding them out even as he thrust upward against her still hips and came along with her….

MATT AWAKENED, FEELING better than he had in a long, long time. His neck hurt, his arm was asleep, but nestled in his arms was his wife, making any discomfort worth it.

He burrowed his nose into her hair and took a deep breath. It was funny how it was the little things he missed the most about her. How she smelled in that little stretch of skin just behind her ear. The line of her jaw. The curve of her heel. The soft, almost sighlike sound she made while she slept.

He cuddled her closer, reveling in the crush of her bottom against his semiarousal, the memory of their lovemaking setting him on fire all over again. It was as if they'd tried to make up for the past year and a half in one night. They hadn't finally fallen asleep until sometime after six in the morning, the winter skies still dark, the chill invading even the warm cocoon they had made. He'd reluctantly gotten up and built a fire that would see them through till morning.

Now he guessed it was somewhere around seven, seven-thirty, and he heard footfalls on the stairs. One of the kids, no doubt. He made sure Ana and he were covered and kept his gaze on the entry that bore no door. Lola came into view, a huge pink robe tucked around her. She stared at her parents on the couch then made a face.

"Oh, gross," she said.

She continued on toward the kitchen.

Matt chuckled quietly, not quite ready to let his wife go just yet, no matter how disgusted their oldest child was by the display.

"What is it?" Ana whispered.

"Lola's up."

"Oh, God."

She hurried to get up, but Matt held her firmly in place.

"Let me go," she said. "I've got to get dressed." She looked around. "Where's my nightgown?"

"I have no idea."

Ana hit him in the arm. "Some help you are."

"Lola?" he called.

Her head appeared in the doorway. "What?"

"Let your mother borrow your robe for a minute, will you?"

She made a tsking sound, but took the apparel in question off, revealing the footed pajamas she wore underneath. She handed the robe to her mother who snatched it from her hands.

"I'm never going to be able to sit on that couch again," Lola mumbled as she headed back into the kitchen.

Ana wriggled from Matt's hold and put the robe on, giving him a brief flash of her delectable body before covering it up again.

She sighed. "We're never going to hear the end of this, you know?"

He caressed her breast through the thick terry cloth. "I know."

She batted his hand away, but not in the joking, lighthearted manner in which he was used to.

Uh-oh.

Why did he get the impression that despite their lovemaking, their disagreement was far from settled?

"Get up. Teresa should be dropped off at any moment."

He curved his hands under the back of his head, watching as she searched for her nightgown and panties.

"At least put your pajama bottoms back on," she whispered harshly as she lifted the blanket to find him ready, willing and able.

"I'd prefer to go upstairs with you and take up where we left off."

"Like that's going to happen." She found her nightgown, but had no luck with the panties. "If one of the kids finds them before me, I'll just die."

Matt reached under him and pulled the scrap of material out. She snatched them from his grip and rushed toward the hall and the stairs beyond.

Lola appeared in the entryway again, eating a piece of toast. "You guys aren't, you know, going to make a habit of…that, are you?"

Matt grinned at her.

She rolled her eyes, said something about parents' deranged behavior, and then disappeared back into the kitchen again.

TERESA RETURNED HOME at nine on the button. By that time, Matt had grabbed a shower in the main bathroom, dressed in a fresh T-shirt and jeans, and recruited all three kids to help him with breakfast in the kitchen. Lola was in charge of pancakes, Johnny got sausage and bacon duty and little Tete handled the toast and setting of the table.

Meanwhile, he took care of homemade hash browns and eggs made to order for everyone.

Someone had switched on the radio to a hip-hop station and he asked Tete to turn the channel, directing her to stop at an oldies station. All the kids groaned, but joined in singing shortly thereafter, spoons, spatulas and orange juice containers serving as microphones. Matt picked up Lola to move her out of the way, and sparred with Johnny, and put Tete on the kitchen island to pretend to peel her along with the other spuds.

While there might not have been any waving flags at the airfield or running hugs upon his arrival, this time with his family…this was what it was all about. Mixed in with "hand me this" or "put this on the table" were questions about school and boyfriends and girlfriends and homework, with each holding the other's feet to the fire if they were anything less than honest.

He had good kids. He knew that. He also knew he was blessed. He heard so many stories from fellow marines of their kids' struggles: rehab stints and arrests and school expulsions. Watched them torture themselves with the knowledge that they were powerless to keep any of it from happening.

Next year Lola would be going to OSU, and Johnny was already prepping for his SATs and Teresa would already be going to middle school.

Where did the time go? It seemed he'd blinked and his kids had grown up, two of them practically adults.

He looked toward the kitchen door again for the fifth time in as many minutes. Ana had yet to show up after she left him on the couch in the family room. Where was she? Maybe she'd gone back to sleep. Lord knew he'd thought about it. After last night…well, he could understand if she needed some recuperation time.

He turned the two fried eggs in the pan onto a plate and handed it to a waiting Tete.

"Hey, Mom," Johnny said.

Matt grinned and turned to watch her kiss him on the cheek, then Lola and Teresa.

"Just in time," he said, waiting for his kiss. "Breakfast is just about done."

She avoided his block and went to the refrigerator where she grabbed one of those diet drinks and then fished an energy bar from the cupboard. "Smells good, but I have classes today."

Matt's grin slipped.

"Dad, the pan," Johnny said.

He looked to find the pan smoking. He switched off the flame and removed it from the burner. "Class?" he repeated.

Ana gave him a long look. "Classes. I'm teaching four sessions today, staring at noon."

"Good. Then you have plenty of time for breakfast."

She smiled at him, but there was no warmth in the expression. "Sorry, but I have some errands to run."

"She's always teaching classes," Tete said and gave an exaggerated eye roll.

Ana nudged her with an elbow and then kissed the top of her head. "You've got basketball and swimming practice today, so I wouldn't get to see much of you anyway."

She walked toward the door. "Enjoy your breakfast."

"Wait," Matt said, grabbing a towel and walking toward her as he wiped his hands. "What time will you be back?"

She avoided meeting his gaze as she tucked the bar into her purse and shrugged. "I don't know. Five or six."

"What about dinner?"

Something flashed in her eyes. "Order in. The kids always do."

And then she was gone.

Suddenly the yellow kitchen didn't seem all that sunny anymore.

A FEW HOURS LATER Matt was ready to jump out of his skin. He and the kids had finished breakfast and seen to clean-up. Then Lola had taken Teresa to her basketball practice, and she was going to put in a few hours where she worked at a local restaurant, while Johnny left to meet up with his friends at a hockey rink.

He'd fully expected things to be different this time around, but he hadn't exactly imagined they'd be this different. Before he'd been called back to action, the family had spent more time at home together than they'd spent outside. He spent the next couple hours seeing to chores that needed doing around the house. He tightened the lose doorknob on the upstairs bathroom, fixed the slow drip in the downstairs sink, and took the Christmas lights down.

But no matter what he did, he couldn't seem to drown out the silence of the house.

So just after noon he climbed into his car and drove to his brother's house on the other side of town.

"Matt!" Ramon welcomed him with a bear hug and hearty back pat. "What the hell you doing back early?"

Matt entered the house and Ramon looked behind him. "Where's Ana?"

"Working."

"Working?"

Matt shrugged out of his coat and hung it on the nearby coat tree. "Funny, I was going to ask what you knew about it."

Ramon shook his head. "I don't know anything. Maybe Pilar does."

Ramon led the way into the kitchen at the back of the house where the couple and their two kids were having a lunch of soup and sandwiches. Pilar immediately got him a bowl as the kids welcomed him back.

"Yes, Ana told me about it," she admitted. "Said she was going stir-crazy at the house by herself all day."

"Why didn't you say anything to me?" Ramon asked.

"I did. But if it doesn't have anything to do with money or an emergency, you don't hear half of what I say."

"That's not true." Ramon gave Matt a long-suffering look.

Matt scratched his head with both of his hands. "I know what she means about going stir-crazy. The house emptied out by ten with no one due back until around dinnertime and I almost broke that old clock in the hall because the ticking was driving me crazy."

"So you decided to come over here and drive us nuts instead," Ramon offered.

Matt was too preoccupied to respond in the joking way he might have otherwise. "Something like that."

Long seconds passed. Matt finally looked up and caught Ramon and Pilar exchanging a glance.

"Hey, little brother, is everything okay?"

"Huh?" Matt looked at the kids who thankfully were fighting over who had spilled the mustard. "Yeah, yeah, I'm fine."

But his family wasn't. And for the life of him, he didn't know what to do about that.

4

IF MATT FOUND THE HOUSE unbearably empty before, now he found it overcrowded as the day he was originally scheduled to return dawned and the party Ana had arranged came together. All morning deliveries were being made and arrangements were being finalized, the women of the family popping up to put this in the oven to keep warm, or that in the refrigerator to keep cold. All three kids had friends over to help them with decorations.

If he found it ironic that the party organizers pretty much ignored him though the party was in his honor, he wasn't telling anyone. All he'd probably get for his efforts anyway would be an eye roll and a smart-ass comment like, "Get real, Dad."

Ana was so busy he barely had the chance to talk to her.

Not that it mattered. The past two days had been pure torture as he'd watched her come and go with barely a look in his direction. He was floored that the same woman who had snuck under his blanket in the family room now looked like she might walk over that same blanket with little concern for what might lie beneath.

"Is there anything I can do to help?" he asked as Lola walked past him with a tray of finger foods to take into the dining room, which had been transformed into the buffet center.

The expected eye roll and then: "You're not even supposed to be here yet, so just find a place to chill."

Funny, but her words could have summed up his entire experience since coming home early: he wasn't really there.

He tried to trap Ana in the pantry, his intentions not all about conversation. Especially when he saw the tell-tale leap of her pulse at the base of her long, graceful neck.

"Why is it I feel invisible, Ana?" he whispered, taking the pie she held in her hands and putting it on a shelf of canned vegetables.

She gasped as he grazed his lips along that same neck.

"Well, what do you expect? You're the one who's been gone for the past fourteen months, Mateo. And you leave again in what? A little over three weeks? You're taking a vacation while for everyone else, this is our lives."

"Vacation? This doesn't look like any vacation I can remember taking."

God, she tasted so good. And he'd kissed her so little since he'd been back.

She pushed him away and quickly gained her freedom through the pantry door. "Maybe I should say you're a visitor then."

Matt stared after her.

A visitor in his own home.

He picked up the pie and followed in Ana's footsteps, trying to digest her words.

THE ACHE IN ANA'S CHEST seemed to grow larger with each passing second. As she took items one by one out of the refrigerator, the final touches on the dinner buffet, she snuck a look at Mateo, who sat on the stairs leading upstairs. He had his powerful hands clasped between his knees and seemed to be staring at them without really seeing them.

She hadn't meant what she'd said to him. Well, not completely. And she certainly hadn't meant to say the words on the night of his welcome-home party. But he'd backed her up against the wall, literally, and she'd lashed out with but a few of the words she'd planned to say to him once tonight was out of the way and they finally had the talk that had been years in coming.

God, he looked so incredibly hurt. His handsome face was drawn into long lines. Never had she seen her Mateo look so out of sorts. As if he didn't know where he belonged.

Good, a part of her said. Maybe by experiencing what she felt every time he walked out that door not to return for over a year, he might understand what she had to say to him.

Yet another part wanted to go to him and put her hands on either side of his head and kiss the sadness out of his big, dark eyes.

Her life recently had emerged a seesaw of sorts, coming down one way, then thunking to the other. She had no idea what Matt faced when he was away. He'd never been one to bring his battles home. But she knew that it couldn't be pretty. Days of one-hundred-and-twenty degree desert heat. Sandstorms that choked the air off. IEDs (improvised explosive devices also known as roadside bombs) and snipers and, unique to urban warfare, enemies hiding right in the light of day, much less in the shadows.

But she couldn't help thinking that he had chosen that over the life they had settled into as a family. Had all too eagerly returned to active duty when the call came in.

She knew the alternative was court-martial and possible prison time, but a part of her thought that would have been preferable to what she endured while he was gone.

She also knew that Mateo would never go that route. There wasn't one bone in his body that wasn't true blue, loyal and honorable. It was one of the many qualities that had originally endeared him to her. *This man, he'll love me always,* she'd known from the beginning. And she'd never had cause to doubt his love.

After all this time, and after having sacrificed so much so long ago, she thought it was finally time that she came first.

"I'm thinking about enlisting," Johnny said next to her.

Ana nearly dropped the plate of deviled eggs she held as she turned to stare at her sixteen-year-old son. He wasn't talking to her, but rather was speaking to his uncle Ramon, Matt's brother.

Ramon met her gaze. He must have seen the horror on her face because he quickly put an arm over Johnny's shoulders and led him downstairs where their finished basement served as a rec center of sorts.

Ana put the plate down and grasped the side of the counter, feeling the world tilt under her. She looked up to find Matt staring at her in concern.

It's all your fault, she wanted to say. *It's not enough that you put your own life at risk; now because of the impossible, improbable example you set, our son—my Johnny—wants to follow in your footsteps.*

Matt began to get up. She held up a hand to tell him not to bother, he wouldn't like what she said when he got there, then she took the eggs into the dining room even as the first of the guests arrived.

IF MATT HAD BEEN HOPING the party would mark a true welcoming home, he was sadly mistaken. Long after the trays were covered and put away or sent home with family and friends, nothing but the scent of candles lingering in their wake, things continued on much as they had before the party. Ana was locked in their bedroom upstairs and Matt was camped out on the family-room sofa, which was getting old quick. Despite his less than hospitable sleeping arrangements in Iraq, here he felt worse, like he had a permanent crick in his neck, and he never slept well, waking up several times during the night to turn this way or that, trying to find a comfortable position.

This was ridiculous. He'd pussyfooted around his own house long enough trying to find a way around the problems that refused to go away. It was past time he charged into the fray and faced this battle head-on.

He stripped the blanket from his legs and got up, squinting at the VCR clock. Just past 2:00 a.m. The kids would be long since asleep. So would Ana, for that matter.

But not for long….

He went upstairs, tried the master bedroom door only to find it locked. He'd installed the mechanism himself, had intended the room to be a safe room of sorts, which meant that while getting around the lock wasn't impossible, it would take much more time than he was willing to invest at that point.

So he went around the other way….

It had snowed the night before, making his efforts more treacherous than they normally would have been, but he was barely aware of the ice against his bare feet, much less the risk involved in climbing up the back porch onto the second-floor deck that jutted out from the master bedroom. He hauled himself up and stood outside the balcony doors in his T-shirt and drawstring pants, trying to see inside.

Just as he suspected: Ana hadn't put the safety bar in place. During several family drills when he'd first installed the safety devices, he'd called her out on her carelessness.

"Who would want to climb the back deck, for God's sake, Matt?" she'd protested.

Now he was infinitely glad she was so stubborn, because if she had used the bar, he wouldn't have been able to gain access to the room unless he broke the glass. And even that was shatterproof.

He quietly jiggled the door, pulling it free from the lock, and opened the glass door with a soft whoosh, then closed it behind himself.

He shivered in the dark. Probably he should have put on some shoes and at least a shirt. But he'd been so consumed with the idea of getting to his wife, he'd been unable to concentrate on anything else.

He heard a dull, metallic click and froze.

"Go right back out the way you came, buster, or be prepared to meet your maker."

Since when had Ana become such a light sleeper? There was a time when tornado sirens had proven ineffective against her deep slumber. Now she was not only fully alert, she had somehow managed to get the 9 mm out of the bedside table and had it trained on him.

He couldn't help grinning with pride. Even as he faced the prospect of eating a few pieces of lead.

"Ana, it's me."

No response. Then she dropped her hands and gun to the comforter. "Mateo? What in the hell are you doing breaking into the bedroom?"

He crossed the room, smoothed back her tousled hair, then ran his hand down over her arm to where she still held the gun. He gently extracted it, popped the round out of the chamber, and then put both back into the bedside table drawer, the combination lock clicking closed. He switched the lamp on top to low, throwing the familiar room into subtle relief.

"I want back into our room," he said quietly, pressing his thighs against the side of the mattress and crowding her sitting form to his chest. He entangled his fingers into her soft hair and held her close. "I want things between us to be the way they were before."

Her arms went around his hips, holding tight. "Before when? Before you left?"

He kissed the top of her head. "Yes," he whispered.

She tilted her head up, her dark eyes large and luminous. He groaned, her beauty never failing to steal the ground beneath his feet.

"I don't think that's possible, Matt. I don't think it's possible for us to ever go back to the way we were before."

He searched her face, finding a pain there that he hadn't viewed before. A sadness that she covered with bravado and avoidance. Its presence twisted like a knife to the gut.

"Sure we can, Ana. All we have to do is try."

Her hands pushed up his T-shirt in the back and clenched the fabric in her fists. "I'm afraid it's too late for that."

In all the time he'd been home, all they'd gone through, he'd never once thought that he might lose his wife. He figured that somehow, some way, they'd work through their current problems, just like they'd tackled the ones that had come before.

He grasped her shoulders perhaps a little too tightly. She gasped, staring up at him.

Then he claimed her mouth as he'd been aching to do since the last time they'd kissed.

To his relief, she kissed him back with the same almost desperate need. The mere thought that he might lose her was enough to scare him more than anything an enemy might use against him. It also made him that much more determined to hold on to her. To pull out all the stops to remind her of what they had together. What had always existed between them.

He pulled her to stand up and freed her from her nightgown, skimming the sides of her full breasts as he brought his hands back down to encircle her narrow waist even as she stripped him of his T-shirt and pants. He knew he'd never lose his desire for this one woman. She touched him in ways that couldn't be taught or even voiced. She set his blood ablaze, made him feel like a man capable of anything.

Without her…

He increased the pressure of his mouth against hers, curving his fingers down her back to cup her perfect bottom. He parted her from behind and then picked her up, her legs automatically going around his hips, her hands grasping his shoulders. Her dark hair swung as she sought purchase. Then just as quickly she reached down her stomach to find his rigid shaft and positioned it against the place she obviously needed it most. Matt gritted his back teeth to sand as she slowly slid down his length….

5

ANA LOVED HER HUSBAND more than she could bear. No matter what she did or said, nothing seemed capable of changing that. She might be able to ignore it, to keep herself busy enough to push it to the back of her mind, but when he kissed her, her love for him took on a life of its own. Everything within her longed to join with everything within him.

It had been the same since they'd first made love years ago. And it would remain the same until the day she died.

She wound her arms around his neck as he thrust upward once…then twice, causing her breasts to bounce against his chest. With every stroke, her temperature rose, her heartbeat increased, and it became more difficult to breathe.

He took his right hand from her butt and raised it to the side of her face, threading his fingers through her hair and then holding her still as he kissed her.

She could get lost in his kiss. Lips searching, tongues tangling, breath mingling, she always felt like she could kiss him forever and never want for anything more. Not food, not water, not clothing. He dropped the hand again and shifted both up her thighs, taking her legs from around his hips and bringing her to a standing position in a way that kept them connected right until her feet hit the ground and her shorter height separated them. He backed her against the bed until she sat down on it. Ana moved backward, her legs together, and he followed her, kneeling in front of her before reaching to part her legs, baring her to his hot gaze.

She swallowed thickly as he dropped a series of leisurely, fiery kisses up the inside of her calf, her knee, her thigh…. By the time he was finally within kissing distance to the throbbing flesh that wanted his attention most, Ana was out of her mind with desire. He gently parted her and pressed his lips against her tight bud. Her hips automatically bucked from the mattress and up against him as she exploded into a spicy red-hot cloud.

Matt didn't retreat. Instead, he heightened her orgasm, pulling the hooded flesh into his mouth and suckling it. Ana was sure she'd never stop quaking, never stop shuddering. She arched her back, shamelessly pressing herself even harder against him.

Finally, she collapsed against the bed, trying to find her breath, her skin covered in a light sweat. Just when she believed she might recover, he thrust into her to the hilt, robbing her of freedom of will all over again.

Ana was convinced that one of the most beautiful sights in the world was watching her husband make love to her. He did so with his gaze full on her, with such intense concentration and total captivation that it was sometimes easy to believe that they were one person rather than two.

His strokes grew deeper, longer, and she stretched her body to help. Up and up she flew, feeling him right there with her, until they both came together in a flash of blinding light.

But this time when Ana came down, she crashed as if she'd leapt from the top of a forty-foot building and there was nothing to cushion her fall….

MATT WAS RENDERED completely helpless as Ana clutched at him, a sob escaping her throat. He tried to get her to look at him, but she refused the action, her tears soaking the front of his chest.

"Ana, please…talk to me, baby."

She appeared to try, but each time was cut off by renewed crying. "I…I can't do this anymore, Mateo. I just can't."

Panic filled his chest as he sat back on his feet and gathered her close. One moment they'd been joined together, making love, the next she was crying as if the world was minutes from coming to an end.

And maybe it was.

She finally looked into his face and what he saw etched on hers sent ice skating down his back.

"Ever since you went back…I've been so scared. All those men…all those families that lost sons, fathers, husbands…" She began shaking her head and tears stopped her words again.

"Shh," Matt told her, holding her close.

He knew what she was talking about. Spent large amounts of time trying to keep from thinking of the tragedy himself. Within a short time span, his reserve company had suffered the greatest loss of any single company so far in the war. Over sixty-five percent of their men had returned home in flag-draped coffins.

"I wake up in the middle of the night, my heart beating so hard I'm afraid I'm going into cardiac arrest," Ana whispered, searching his face. "I think of that all the time, waiting for your phone call to tell me you're okay. I dream that you're in one of those awful caskets and that I…that I'm never going to see you again."

It was a reality that every military family with a member in a war zone experienced. It wasn't unique to them.

"In the beginning…when we first got married, I could handle it," Ana said. "It was just the way things were. You went off to Bosnia and I stayed here to take care of the kids. I knew the odds, the risks, but I was able to cope. Now…"

She began shaking her head again.

"I can't do it anymore, Matt. I just can't. I've even cut off most contact with other military wives. Their fear only seems to amplify mine. And I no longer have any words of encouragement to give them. No matter how hard I try…no matter what I do…I'm just so damn scared of losing you…"

"Oh, baby," he murmured into her hair. "It's all right. I promise you, nothing's going to happen. I only have a year left before I can transfer back stateside. We can get through this. Really, we can."

But for the first time, he began to fear, like her, that they wouldn't….

Two days later, Ana was physically at the dance studio, but emotionally she was still at home, staring at Matt from across the kitchen table. Ever since the night she'd confessed her fears, they'd spent untold amounts of time together. Not talking. Just touching. Whether it was at night when they made silent love, or during the day when they sat for hours holding each other's hands on the sofa in the family room while the kids watched TV, a sense of growing dread had settled over them.

A fear that she couldn't remember seeing Matt feel before.

"We're not young anymore, Matt," she'd told him that night. "I can't handle it the way some of the newly-weds can. Day by day I can feel myself shutting off from you. From our marriage. To protect myself. To protect our children…"

She'd just finished with a class and the next didn't start for another hour. She stood clutching the bar, her eyes tightly closed, mouthing the words that reran through her mind.

What had she done?

One of the first things she'd determined her first time around as a military wife was that she would never, ever show her husband her fear. To do so would be to put his mind on other things and not on the job in front of him. To distract him was to doom him, to make him little more than a moving target for his enemies.

If his mind was back home, it wasn't on what he had…no, needed to do to stay alive.

Dear Lord, what had she done?

It suddenly struck her that she'd allowed her own fear to precipitate exactly what she'd been afraid of: losing Matt.

She clutched the bar tighter, battling back the dread that threatened to overwhelm her, the shame that was beginning to rear its ugly head, and the fear that she'd done irreparable damage to her marriage.

"Ana?"

She stilled, sure she'd imagined his voice. But she felt his presence strong and rocklike behind her.

She turned, her heart expanding to fill her chest. "Mateo."

She searched his face, taking a mental inventory of the damage she'd done. Not just to him, but to herself.

He came toward her, his expression serious, his movements slow.

"I want you to teach me," he said quietly, coming to stand just in front of her.

She blinked, only semiaware of the CD that continued to play the rumba rhythms she'd put on after the last class.

"You want me to...to teach you how to dance?"

He shook his head, then nodded. "No...and yes." He took her right hand and then pulled her to him. "I want you to teach me how to help you through this. I want you teach me the steps back to your fearless heart. I want you to tell me how to save our marriage."

She held his hand so tightly, squeezed his shoulder so hard, that she was surprised he didn't wince.

"I want you to assure me that everything is going to be okay," he whispered into her ear.

She began the dance. One foot, then two. Front and then back. Swaying her hips away from him and then toward him, holding his gaze fast.

It wasn't until that one moment that she understood that everything would be all right. No matter what happened. She loved this man. He loved her. They loved their family.

Nothing...not a war, not time apart, not fear, could ever change that....

Justice

1

BRIAN JUSTICE STEPPED OFF the bus from Pensacola along with other countless, nameless military personnel catching a ride home to the Ballard Armory in Miami, Florida. The crowd of relatives waiting behind a barricade surged forward, invading the open space, throwing themselves into the arms of brothers, sisters, husbands, wives and lovers. Kids were swept up into the air, babies were placed in the arms of new fathers, and military mothers crowded their children close.

Brian focused his attention toward escape. No one was waiting for him at the organized event. His parents were probably at the country club near their mansion in Palm Beach, aware of his arrival, but determined not to do anything to commemorate it. To do so would be to imply that either of them believed there was merit in his decision not to join the family company but instead enlist in the military. It didn't matter that he was a decorated marine officer. His father forever waited for the day when he'd come to his senses and realize that the real test of a man's metal wasn't in war, but on the corporate battlefield.

Then there was Vanessa...

A cold numbness swept over him, the same type of sensation he experienced when he faced off with an enemy, guns loaded and aimed at each other.

Vanessa was his college sweetheart. A woman more beautiful than anyone had a right to be. Their families went way back, and while he'd been familiar with her growing up, they'd never clicked until they were older. She was polished elegance and practiced charm. And she'd brought him to his knees with plenty of hot sex. Until one morning he'd told her that rather than going on to Oxford for postgraduate studies from the Ivy League university they attended as they'd both planned, he had instead enrolled in the Officer Candidate Course at the Marine Corps base in Quantico.

She'd left his bed and his life, telling him that if he ever came to his senses, he had her number. But not to call her until he woke from whatever demented dream he was having.

Now, Brian sidestepped an army grunt hoisting a busty brunette up into his arms, barely avoiding taking an elbow to the eye. Give him a neighborhood full of insurgents and urban combat over a tarmac full of sentimental military families any day.

He rounded what looked like the entire extended family of another fellow marine and stopped cold before a kid that looked like he was maybe nine or ten, with orange-red hair, big blue eyes and freckles standing out brightly on his round, pale face…and was staring directly up at him.

"Welcome back, soldier," the boy said, thrusting his hand forward.

Brian squinted at him and then looked around for who the kid might be meeting. His father, maybe? Perhaps even his mother. He looked down again to find he still stubbornly held out his hand to him.

"Sorry, kid, wrong guy."

A soft, unfamiliar feminine laugh. "Actually, you appear to be the man he's looking for."

The boy looked up at the woman standing behind him. Brian followed his lead…and suddenly felt as if he'd just taken a rifle butt to the solar plexus.

She had glossy black hair and violet eyes, and the way she smiled at the boy and then him seemed to rival the midday Miami sun, which was quite a task, but one she was up for.

Without realizing he was going to do it, Brian slowly extended his hand. The boy took it and shook it like he'd been practicing the move for days. "Welcome home, soldier," he said again.

The woman cleared her throat. "Actually, the correct address would be, 'Welcome home, Marine.'"

"Your mom's right, kid."

"She's not my mom. She's Miss Mitchell."

Five other kids around the boy's age crowded around her, three girls holding what looked like daisies. "Hi. I'm Angela Mitchell. I'm a counselor at Harbor's."

She'd extended her own hand and he automatically took it. Small. Soft. So incredibly soft. And warm. Her fingertips brushed against his wrist and Brian was reminded of how very long he'd gone without a woman's touch. How long since he'd even thought about the opposite sex? He'd been so preoccupied with the court-martial hanging over his head like a swinging noose he hadn't had time to think of much else.

But standing there looking into Angela Mitchell's bedroom eyes made him feel like he'd spent the past year thinking about her.

She didn't seem immune to the attraction that arced between them as she dropped her gaze and licked lips that were full and plump and custom-made for kissing.

A girl of about ten thrust wilted flowers at him. "We're looking for a few good men."

The girl's words caught him up short. Not that he had anything to say to the ragtag bunch to begin with, but if he'd had, then her proclamation would have stopped the words. At the very least, it halted whatever was happening between him and Angela.

"And women," she added, looking at him a little too closely.

Brian Justice hadn't spent much time around kids. As an only child, his parents had made sure they insulated him from the world. But he had seen women whose main goal in life was to marry a military officer. It was something about the uniform, some said. Others theorized it was because of the amount of time the men were away from home. But fellow marine Mateo Guerrero had once said he believed it was the romance of it all that enticed women to fall for military men. Tearful partings. Extended separations. Passionate returns. The drama of life multiplied by a hundred.

Which category did Angela Mitchell fit into?

Not that it mattered. He wasn't sticking around to find out.

"Like I said, wrong guy," Brian said quietly, edging around the small gathering.

EXACTLY THE RIGHT GUY.

Angela felt like a garden of butterflies had invaded her stomach as she watched the tall, broad-shouldered marine try to sidestep Oscar. Oscar moved back into his path, denying him passage, his red hair not just signaling high spirits, but a stubbornness that often got him into trouble.

She tucked her chin into her chest to hide her smile.

She spotted another lone military member walking around the reunited families like a ghost. She pointed him out to the kids and they descended on the poor guy like a pack of excited puppies.

Except for Oscar. Oz stayed, staring up at the marine as if trying to figure out if he was really as tall as he was…and whether or not he would ever be that big.

Wounded Heroes: U.S. military personnel returning home with psychological wounds as critical as physical injuries.

The headline was splashed across a magazine cover that had caught Angela's attention a couple months ago. She'd bought the periodical and had pored over the extended piece countless times, reading stories of soldiers with extreme cases of PTSD—post-traumatic stress disorder—returning home ill-equipped to reenter civilian life.

The accounts of marines with no family had especially touched her. The men reminded her so much of her children. Orphans who had seen more than their own fair share of domestic warfare and acted out in ways big and small.

She'd thought if she could somehow, some way bring the two factions together, maybe, just maybe, they could help each other.

"I brought the kids over to welcome home those who appeared to be without families," she said, drawn in by the wary shadow in the marine's eyes. "We didn't mean to offend."

"No offense, ma'am."

"It's miss… I'm sorry. I didn't catch your name."

"Captain Justice. Brian Justice."

"That's not really your name," Oscar said.

Brian looked down at him. "Unfortunately, it is."

"It's an honor to make your acquaintance, Captain Justice."

He stared at her, as if he couldn't figure out what to make of her.

She shivered at the open appraisal. Then she realized it was because he was looking at her mouth rather than her eyes.

She licked her lips.

"Harbor's is a home for kids in transit."

"It's an orphanage," Oz said.

Angela rested her hand on his shoulder and squeezed. "I thought it might be a good idea for me to bring a few of them over to help welcome back our military members."

"Thank you, Miss Mitchell...and Oscar." He looked down at Oz as if he hadn't been aware humans came in that size.

"You're welcome, Marine," Oz said.

Oscar raised his hand in a salute. Angela coughed, having warned him not to salute anyone. Marines, especially, were sticklers for protocol.

To her surprise, Justice's posture changed and he returned the salute.

She smiled, blinking up into his face. A wide, strong face with sharp brown brows, hazel eyes and a jawline that a woman could spend an entire night exploring with her tongue.

She caught her wandering thoughts and bent down to talk into Oz's ear. "Why don't you go catch up with everyone else while I talk to Captain Justice?"

He looked up at her. "Yes, ma'am," he mimicked the marine.

Angela laughed, half afraid he was going to salute her. He didn't, but he did do as she requested and caught up with the other kids, who had finished greeting lost returns and were ducking in between and climbing the fence that served as a barricade.

She sighed. "I'd adopt them all if I could."

Justice shifted on his feet as if uncomfortable. "Well, thank you for the sentiment, Miss Mitchell. I'm sure the men flying solo appreciate it."

She touched his arm as he began to pass. "But not you?"

His arm was rip-cord hard under the material of his khaki shirt and she was suddenly aware of how very tall he was. At five-seven, she wasn't exactly on the short side, but standing next to him she almost felt petite. No small feat.

"The little girl said you were looking for a few good men?" he asked, then appeared to regret it.

"That would be Lauren. Whatever is inside her head tends to come straight out of her mouth."

A bit of a smile.

Her heart skipped a beat and she suddenly felt hot all over. A reaction that had less to do with the warm, January day in southern Florida, and more to do with the hot marine.

"I'm…the center, rather, is looking for a few men to act as big brothers to a couple of the boys."

"Oscar?"

She smiled and crossed her arms over her cotton shirt. "Yes, Oz is one. His father's never really been in the picture and his mom's been in and out of rehab so many times that the state finally took full custody of him just before Christmas. He's been…" She caught her bottom lip between her teeth, remembering the night sweats and rebellious acts. "He's having a harder time adjusting than some of the other kids."

"And you think I can help."

It was a statement more than a question.

Angela looked at him for a long moment. She'd been hoping to find men like him. Perhaps a little more social, comfortable around kids, but...

"Yes. Yes, I think maybe you can."

BRIAN STOOD AT THE WOOD railing of his modest deck that jutted out over the dunes and overlooked the Atlantic Beach. His two-bedroom bungalow might be small by his family's standard—hell, they had two guest houses on their West Palm Beach property that were three times bigger than his place—but it was home to him in a way that the twenty-three-thousand-foot mansion where his parents still lived had never been. First, he knew where to find everything. Second, everything he wanted was at his fingertips.

Despite its small size, however, it was a luxury that few of his fellow marines could afford. The beach location alone priced the place out of a great many people's reach. The towering condos just up the beach went for seven figures.

But his financial viability merely by being a member of the Justice family was currently lost on him. Right now he was wondering what in the hell he was going to do to occupy his time until the hearing two weeks away.

Court-martial...

Brian rubbed the back of his neck. Just thinking the words made him feel clammy all over. The possibility that he might serve time in a military prison didn't bother him as much as the chance that they might strip him of his commission.

While he'd always done well in school, and his reasons for originally enrolling in the OCC had more to do with rebellion than any strong sense of duty, he'd immediately felt he'd found his calling among the men and women of the Corps. It didn't matter where they came from, what their fathers' names were, they were judged strictly on their ability to perform well under pressure of combat. Never had he felt so alive than when training, becoming not only physically sharper than he'd ever been, but mentally, as well.

Simply, he'd just fit.

And the possibility of having all that stripped away from him ripped his guts out.

He stared out at the sparkling turquoise of the Atlantic Ocean, spotting a couple of surfers catching a winter wave. Maybe that's what he'd do. Or maybe he'd go check on his thirty-two-foot boat docked at a nearby intercoastal marina.

Neither possibility appealed to him enough to act on.

Instead, what continued to come to mind no matter how much he fought it was Miss Angela Mitchell's open, pretty face. More, the luscious body she hid under the nondescript cotton of her T-shirt and jeans. It had been a good, long while since he'd lost himself in the scent of a woman.

"I know the thought of jumping right in might seem a little overwhelming at first," she'd said, when he'd insisted he wasn't the man she was looking for to spend time with her kids. "So why don't you come for dinner?"

"Like at a mess hall with all the children?" he'd asked.

Her sexy smile had mesmerized him. "No, like at my apartment. I bet it's been a while since you've had a nice, home-cooked meal."

He hadn't said anything.

"I make a helluva key lime pie from scratch."

He'd nearly taken her up on her invitation right then and there. The only homemade pie he'd ever eaten had come from Marta, the Justice family cook. The concept of eating a piece made by someone not under his employ intrigued him.

"Here," she'd said, taking a card out of her back pocket. "Do you have a pen?"

He produced one and she'd scribbled on the back of the card.

"This is my phone number and my address. I'll go ahead and make the pie. Call or stop by at any time after six in the next couple of days and I promise you a meal you won't soon forget."

Brian squinted at a boat cutting through the waters a few hundred yards out. He was completely convinced that Angela would make good on her promise. And even suspected that if he turned on a bit of the Justice charm, he'd get her to give him much more than pie.

The mere thought of cupping her full breasts and kissing her sexy mouth was enough to make him try to remember where he'd left her card.

The problem lay in that women like Angela didn't do casual.

She'd gone to the armory to recruit men to mentor her boys. So any sex he had with her would come with strings attached.

Which was exactly why he was going to go sailing instead.

2

ANGELA WASHED THE FEW DISHES in the sink of her small apartment and put them in the drainer. She dried her hands and looked at her watch. Just after eight o'clock and she'd just given up on Captain Brian Justice for the second night in a row.

Of course, trying to recruit him had been a long shot. But it wasn't the professional letdown that occupied her thoughts. While the nature of her occupation made it virtually impossible to separate her job from her personal life—it was hard to leave the kids' laughter and struggles at work—she didn't think her borderline obsession with seeing Justice again had anything to do with watching him teach Oscar how to play basketball.

She caught herself caressing the side of her neck, but stopped short of pulling her hand away here in the privacy of her apartment. Other rules applied in public. It seemed that every moment of the past day and a half since she'd met Justice at the armory she'd been hyperaware of herself as not only a woman, but as a woman who wanted one man in particular. He was never far from her thoughts, no matter what she was doing and she found her mind wandering to what it might be like to kiss his firm mouth. To touch him in a way that would tear down his hard composure, destroy his rigid control. To welcome him into her body.

Her foster mother had always told her she was a dreamer. And it hadn't always been meant in a flattering way. She'd get marked down in classes for daydreaming, and would take forever doing dishes because she was looking out the window envisioning a different life, another world. Looking back, it wasn't all that difficult to understand why. Spending her teenage years in a double-wide with five other foster children often inspired flights of fancy when she'd lain across her top bunk and stared at the grainy photos she'd clipped out of free papers and taped to the ceiling. While her foster sisters favored glossy posters of Leonardo DiCaprio and The Backstreet Boys, her collection was of families, children, wildlife and sunsets. Her diary was full of teenage meanderings on the man she might meet and the life she might lead once she was an adult. And she'd had to protect the romance novels she'd checked out of the library because her foster siblings' favorite way to tease her was to hide her books. She'd been reduced to tears when her overcharge fees had hit five dollars at one point and she'd had no way to pay them, which meant she couldn't check out more books. Thankfully the librarian had deleted the charge with a push of a key, but asked that she be more careful.

Now books were piled on nearly every surface in her small, one-bedroom apartment and her choice of photos were in frames and hung on the walls.

Angela opened the refrigerator door to put away the plate of leftovers. The homemade key lime pie was on the top shelf. The sight filled her with longing. She'd taken great joy in making it the day before. A Norah Jones CD had been playing, a light, tropical breeze had been blowing in through the second-floor balcony doors, and hope that Captain Brian Justice would visit had been high.

"I don't know if this big brother project is a good idea," Harbor's director Marsha Nielson had said to her when she'd first proposed taking the kids to greet returning military personnel.

"I don't understand," Angela had said in response.

Marsha had given her a long look. "Listen, Angela. You're great with these kids. But I've warned you before about becoming too emotionally attached."

She'd looked away.

"Trust me, I've been there. Everyone who works here has. Maintaining a professional distance is not only good for you, but for the kids, as well."

"What does this have to do with the big brother project?"

Marsha had sighed and sat back in her office chair, considering her. "These guys returning home from the front...I'm afraid they're not much different than these kids. If you can't keep your professional life separate from your personal with them..."

She hadn't needed to continue. Marsha might have ultimately given her the okay, but it was clear that the director thought it was a mistake.

Angela realized she still held the refrigerator door open and began to close it. Then she changed her mind, taking the pie out and putting it on the small kitchen table before getting a knife and a fork out of the silverware drawer, and a plate from the cupboard. Her interest in Captain Brian Justice had nothing to do with the kids. This was strictly personal. And just because she was having a piece didn't mean she was giving up hope. It meant that she was hungry and the tangy meringue pie would hit the spot just then.

She cut herself a small slice, then changed her mind and cut a bigger one. She transferred it to the plate and sat staring at it for long moments before finally taking a bite. Then another. Flavor exploded on her tongue and she hummed.

The intercom buzzer sounded. She jumped, her fork clattering to the table. Still chewing, she stepped into the hall.

"Yes?"

Silence.

She frowned. Sometimes visitors for other residents in the six-unit building pushed the wrong button.

She started to let go of the button that allowed her to hear when a male voice said, "I'm looking for Angela Mitchell."

Angela's heart skipped a beat. "Um, this is she." She hadn't depressed the right button and had to repeat the sentence, this time without the hesitation.

"This is Brian. Brian Justice."

Oh, God. It was him.

Angela looked down at her white shorts and pink spaghetti-strapped top and then rolled her eyes. She knew what she was wearing. She'd chosen it with the thought that he might be stopping by.

Now she wondered if she should change.

She realized she'd left him waiting. She told him the apartment number and then buzzed him in. Then she opened the door a crack and rushed to her bedroom where she flung open the closet door and took out a sundress. A casual blue one with muted yellow flowers.

"Hello?"

She was midway through stripping off her shorts and hopped toward the bedroom door and opened it slightly. "Come on in. I'll just be a minute."

She leaned the door closed and finished stripping, then pulled the dress over her head. A couple of fluffs to her hair, a quick kicking of the discarded clothes into the closet, and she hurried into the other room, slightly out of breath. Thankfully Justice had his back to her from where he stood in the kitchen doorway. He wore a pair of jeans and green polo shirt.

"Be careful, Angela," had been Marsha's final words to her.

It startled her that she should remember them now.

"You started without me," Brian said quietly.

He'd heard her come out of the room.

Of course he'd heard her. He was trained for stuff like that.

"You're late."

He turned to face her and Angela lost her breath all over again.

She'd forgotten how tall he was. And how strikingly handsome. His gaze was intense and she got the immediate impression that he could see right through her.

She smoothed her skirt, just realizing she hadn't put on shoes as he looked at her feet.

"Mmmm. Hot pink," he said.

She self-consciously dug her toes into the area rug even as he neared her, picking up her right hand and examining her fingernails. She had a simple French manicure she'd done herself.

"Um, are you hungry?" she asked, sliding her hand from his and walking around him toward the kitchen. "I saved a plate. Clam linguine."

Her heart tripped in her chest and her palms were wet.

"Not for linguine."

The low hum of his voice told her he was hungry for

something entirely different. Something having nothing to do with food and everything to do with her.

Why had she not considered that the dynamic between them would change when in the close confines of her apartment? She should have invited him to a public place. Here…here, her entire life was on display, bared, and she felt more than a little vulnerable. Gone was the light humor she'd relied on at the armory. In its absence the attraction she felt for him expanded to engulf her entire body.

She cleaned crumbs from the table, searching for something to say. A response that wouldn't make her sound too horribly stupid. He stepped closer to her backside. She swore she could feel his heat penetrate his clothes and hers.

He reached around her, the inner part of his arm brushing the outer part of hers as he dragged his index finger in the lime part of the pie and then slowly moved it to his mouth. The sucking sound and hum of appreciation seemed too close to her ear. She shivered, her toes curling for an entirely different reason.

"This is what I came for," he said quietly.

He could have as easily been referring to her as the pie.

Angela decided to focus on the pie.

She moved from between him and the table and collected a fresh plate and fork. She turned to find him holding the knife.

"Awfully big instrument for such a small task, don't you think?"

"Whatever gets the job done."

He grinned and then handed the knife to her handle-first.

"Please…sit," she said.

He pulled out the other chair and did as requested.

Angela knew an immediate flush of relief. So long as he was standing he seemed to hold some sort of inexplicable power over her.

She poured two glasses of ice water then took the seat across from him and cut him a large slice of pie. She handed it to him and he made a point of touching her fingers as he took it.

Angela met his gaze, finding a sizzling, hypnotic shadow in his hazel eyes. His every move, every comment, seemed to ooze of sexual tension.

But it was something just beyond that shadow that drew her in, urged her closer. A smear of pain. Of uncertainty. Trace evidence of experiences he could never share, she could never understand. An oil spot that came with a large Caution sign. A sign she ignored, instead allowing herself to respond to him, open to him in a way that her mind told her wasn't wise, but that her heart was helpless to prevent.

"So are you on leave?" she asked quietly, picking up her fork, but doing little more than collecting crust crumbs between the tongs. She doubted she could have swallowed just then.

The question was simple enough. But his reaction as he immediately dropped his attention to his pie wasn't. "You make this yourself?" he asked.

"Yes."

"Are you sure?"

She smiled. "Positive. Would you like to see my rolling pin?"

He took a bite, not saying anything for a long moment before his gaze fastened on her mouth. "Mmm. Very good."

Angela took great pleasure in his approval. Even greater pleasure from his interest in her mouth.

She pressed her hand against the side of her throat, wondering if no one had ever made him a pie from scratch before. Where was he from? Were his parents together? Still alive? Did he have brothers and sisters? What about women? Was there a female out there somewhere, who had also slipped on that oil spot that was his soul, waiting for his phone call?

Brian's gaze followed the move of her hand. She stretched her neck, thinking that she should be looking for something else to say. But for the life of her, she could concentrate on little more than watching him slowly eat his pie…and the awareness sliding over her like warm ocean waters.

She'd been with two men in her life. The first had been a high-school disaster, with neither of them knowing much what to do and over with before it had truly begun. The second had been in college and hadn't been much better. In fact, both experiences had left her reluctant to accept dates. She instead focused on her work at the home and side projects like the search for big brothers for the boys.

But now…

Angela couldn't remember a time when she'd been more aware of a man, more drawn to one. Even though a table separated them, she swore she could feel him reaching for her. Everywhere his gaze fell, a small blaze followed. Her breasts seemed to swell and she felt a definite dampness between her legs.

But it was his darkness, his unspoken need for an unnameable something that rendered her speechless. Completely helpless to stop what she knew was going to happen.

He cleared his throat. "You, um, have some pie right…" He reached his arm across the table, cupping her chin in his fingers and then rubbing his thumb against the corner of her mouth. When he moved the pad to rest against her lips, she met his gaze, seeing deep in his eyes a need greater than the physical. A need that trumped her need to fight him, to maintain a protective distance.

She parted her lips, allowing him entrance to more than merely her mouth.

And he walked all the way in....

3

A LONG TIME WITHOUT SEX combined with a sexy woman equaled sex.

It was as simple and as complicated at that.

At least that's what Brian tried to convince himself of. If the truth lay a little closer to an almost desperate need to escape his current circumstances, and the only thing and only one capable of doing that was Angela… well, he wasn't anywhere near admitting that.

Brian grasped Angela's hand and led her around the table until she straddled him in his chair. All he knew was a need so deep, so complete, that if he didn't claim Angela's mouth he didn't know what he would do.

Thankfully, she appeared a willing participant. She instantly encircled his neck with her arms and met his kiss easily, without reservation, her expression open and inviting.

Brian wasn't exactly sure why, but he forced his gaze away from hers, perhaps because of the complete honesty—and was that trust?—in her eyes, and concentrated on strictly the physical instead. He thrust his hands up the skirt of her dress, meeting the warm, supple flesh of her outer thighs. He brought her hips forward so that her panty-covered mound sat against his throbbing erection.

And for the first time in weeks he knew one thing and one thing only: his need for the woman in his arms.

He reached behind her, tugging on the tie of the halter dress. It gave easily and the two strips of material covering her full breasts draped down to her waist. Her nipples were large and tight. He took one into his mouth. She tasted better than her pie and that was saying a lot.

She undid the buttons at the top of his polo and then pulled the material out of the waist of his jeans, not stopping until she could pull the shirt up and over his head. She ran her hands over his arms, chest and back. He caught one and pressed her palm against the buttons of his jeans.

She hesitated, searching his face, then appeared to reach some sort of decision he wasn't privy to. Finally, she popped the first button and he sighed in relief, and then in desire as she slid her fingers inside his boxers. A long breath hissed from between his teeth as the back of her knuckles grazed his skin as she found what she was seeking. She curled her fingers around his thick, hard girth, making him shift on the chair.

Brian fought to concentrate on his own actions and switched his attention to her other breast. Angela made a soft sound and her eyelids fluttered closed. Damn, but she was beautiful. It was what had originally drawn his attention to her. But it was not the reason he'd come to her apartment. There was something more about her. She'd seemed to look beyond what was on the surface to the man he was below. She'd seen him. Brian had never quite experienced a moment like that. It was almost as if she'd slid under his skin, taken a look around, and then left a little something behind for him to remember her by. It was the reason he hadn't been able to shake her from his mind despite everything going on.

Not even sailing or surfing or scuba diving had shaken her hold on him.

He moved his hands a little farther up her hot thighs until he met with the elastic of her panties. Cotton. Bikini. Not thong.

He tunneled his fingers under the elastic until he met with the soft, damp curls covering her swollen flesh. No waxing here. The natural state touched off something fundamental within him.

She traded her interest in his neck for his mouth, kissing him softly, kissing him well. He returned the attention, absorbing her gasp when he slid his index finger into her shallow channel, drawing it down, then up to the tiny bit of flesh at the top.

He spoke without breaking contact with her delicious mouth. "Condom…we need a condom…"

"Where?" she whispered.

"Back pocket."

"Which one?"

"Right."

Angela slid her fingers into the pocket in question and came out with a foil packet. Somewhere in the back of his mind, Brian thought that he should rid himself of his jeans, and that she should take off her panties, but that's where the thoughts stayed—in the back of his mind. He didn't want to do anything that might upset the order of things.

He watched as Angela opened the packet and then he stretched his neck and ground his back teeth together as she unrolled the lubricated latex over his throbbing erection.

Too long…it had been far too long since he'd enjoyed a woman's touch….

Before he knew it, he was pushing the crotch of her

panties aside and grabbing her hips, positioning her over him right then and there on the kitchen chair with the overhead light bright above them. He watched a swallow travel the length of her elegant neck and then her mouth fall open as he brought her down to cover him and she sank down to the hilt.

Yes…

She rocked forward and he immediately grabbed her hips, holding her fast, holding her still. He wanted just a moment like that. Her body pulsing around him. The tightness of her slick muscles adjusting to his length and width.

He'd come to understand that there were few things sweeter than the first moments inside a beautiful woman. The promise, the ecstasy, the building of orgasm. He wanted to draw out every moment.

His hips bucked as if on their own accord. Angela made a soft sound and he watched her pupils widen in her violet eyes, her color growing high, her chest heaving with quickened breaths. He captured one of her nipples between his lips and leisurely laved it; he swore he could count the beat of their hearts where they were connected.

Angela shifted despite his hold and licked her lips. "Please," she rasped.

Brian increased his grip, but rather than holding her still, he moved her back and then brought her forward again. She instinctively grabbed his shoulders, bracing herself and holding herself slightly aloft as he moved her hips again.

Through the sensual fog crowding his brain, her scent filled his senses. She wore a light, cotton-candy-like perfume that made his mouth water. Mingling with that was her feminine musk. He leaned in to kiss her neck, running his tongue along the column until he came to her ear. She wore tiny gold earrings that tinkled when he ran his nose under them. Her hair was soft and tickled his face as he closed his eyes, breathing in everything that was her.

Lovely…clean…painfully sexy.

He kissed her deeply. Then he thrust up into her, causing her to moan in a way that appealed to his sense of sound.

Ask any military man what he missed most about being stationed in the Middle East and they'd invariably tell you the scent of a woman. In a place where religion forbade most unsupervised male-female contact and where more than half the women were covered in hijabs, sex wasn't what they put as number one. It was the small things. Even the married guys said they missed their wives' laughs. Seeing them when they went to sleep and when they woke up every morning.

Brian always kept quiet during these exchanges, but he listened closely. It intrigued him that it was the everyday things the men missed. Pancakes on Sunday morning, a cold beer while watching a football game, the smoke of a BBQ grill cooking a big, thick steak. A long ride in their trucks or motorcycles.

But what they always came back to was their simple need of the opposite sex in their lives.

Brian had never really gotten that…until now. He got the feeling that no matter how long he lived, he'd associate this moment with cotton candy, key lime pie and Angela's unique musk.

At her soft sound of protest, he thrust his hips up again…and then again, the pressure in his balls growing to an unbearable degree even as she gasped, her body going still as her muscles contracted around him, squeezing him like a moist, velvet glove.

Finally, he allowed himself release, taking in every emotion flickering on Angela's face as he did so….

"THERE'S A HOSTILE reported operating in the area. Cleanse him out."

The order was a simple one. The plan clear. Justice and his men were to go door-to-door in the Baghdad neighborhood of Adhamiya, which was deathly quiet as everyone waited out the latest incident of violence.

After more than five years of war, the troops and residents moved through incidents like this like clockwork. Doors were either opened or kicked in as the troops went room to room searching out the latest insurgent to upset the fragile peace. Some residents you could count on to steer you toward the hostile, or offer a warning if you were about to walk into an ambush. Others were too scared to say or do anything as they huddled in a corner with their family members, praying for the moment to pass without harm.

It appeared in this house the family was going to be the latter. He nodded to a man gathering his wife, probably his mother, and his three kids in a corner of the living room behind an overturned dining room table. Justice flanked the side of the doorway leading to the back rooms, leading with his M-16 assault rifle as he scanned the kitchen. It appeared empty. He did the same with the hall leading off to the right. Empty, but there were three doors covered with sheets, blocking off a clear view.

After six hours of fruitless searching, Brian knew his team was at risk of one of two reactions: either fatigue would cause them to let their guards down, or, worse, they would be more on edge because each house brought them closer to their target.

He motioned an all clear and then gestured to his men with two fingers to precede him.

"Keep alert," he said in hushed tones as they hustled down the hall, each of them taking position at each of the doors.

Eric Armstrong and Eddie Cash took the farthest door, while Matt Guerrero and Chris Conrad took the second. He knew he didn't have anything to worry about with the first three. It was the fourth, Chris Conrad, that concerned him. The recent transfer had been downing those damn energy drinks like water all day and he virtually vibrated he was so pumped full of caffeine and adrenaline. Brian had told him to knock it off and Conrad's response was to pop the top off another one and hold the can up in a toast, a cocky grin on his sunburned face.

He silently gauged Conrad's readiness now. He was paired with Guerrero, a move Brian had made to try to balance the kid out. While he was the same age as Eddie, he wasn't made of the same stuff. Eddie might appear simple, but when it came to combat situations he had one of the coolest heads in the corps.

In the short time he'd been with the company, Conrad had proven himself trigger-happy and a hothead.

But the time to do anything about that wasn't now. They needed to take care of business and scare this insurgent out of the bushes.

His M-16 assault rifle in his right hand, Brian began counting off with his left to launch a coordinated run on the rooms. Three…two…

A man shouted in Arabic behind him and gunfire exploded before he reached "one." It was all over in ten seconds as Brian crouched closer to the floor, taking in the aftermath through the scope of his M-16.

"Captain, we have a civilian down here," Guerrero shouted.

Brian scanned to his right. They had a civilian down here, too. More specifically, the father that had been in the other room, who had probably come to warn them that another family member was in one of the bedrooms.

Now they were both dead....

Brian woke with a start, his breathing heavy, the image of the twelve-year-old girl's blood-covered face, and the father's unseeing eyes staring up at him in lifeless shock burned forever onto his retinas.

It took a moment to figure out where he was. The unfamiliar room was painted yellow and smelled of lavender, the double bed narrower than his king.

"Shhh," a female voice said and a hand touched his shoulder. "It was just a dream."

Brian looked at Angela in the light that shone from the hall then at the clock. Just past four in the morning.

He wiped the sweat from his brow and began to get up, ignoring her attempts to try to get him to lie back down.

When was the last time he'd fallen so deeply asleep at a woman's place? He couldn't remember, but he was pretty sure it was never.

Why had he done so now?

"You're soaking wet," she said quietly. "Let me go get you some water and a washcloth."

"No," he said, reaching for his pants only to figure out he'd left them in kitchen along with the rest of his clothes. "I've got to go."

"Go where?" she whispered. "It's the middle of the night."

Brian got up from the bed and stalked toward the kitchen, his movements shaky. He'd relived the Adhamiya incident in his sleep no fewer than two times a night since it had happened a little over a month earlier. And it was that incident for which he was facing a court-martial.

He reached the kitchen and got dressed quickly, saving his shoes and socks for last. He sat down to put them on, aware that Angela had slid into a short, silky pink robe and followed him. He ignored her as he finished dressing and then got up and walked toward the doorway where she stood.

He paused slightly, unable to meet her questioning gaze.

"Thanks for the pie," he said, then left the apartment and her behind without a second glance.

4

"Miss Mitchell, is everything all right?"

Angela blinked, banishing the image of Brian's rigid back as he'd walked out of her apartment two nights ago. Despite the warmth of the day, she had her arms wrapped around herself as if warding off a chill.

And she was, wasn't she? The chill of rejection. After she'd opened herself to him. Invited him knowing full well that what had happened would.

She recalled the way he'd jerked awake in the middle of the night. The sweat that had coated him. The edgy, wild-eyed expression on his face, as if fearing the room were filled with enemies and he'd been caught without his gun.

And then he'd shut her down. Refused to even look into her eyes as he'd gotten dressed and left.

Oscar's freckled face came into focus where he was standing in front of her outside the main office of the orphanage. Moments before, he'd been playing kickball with the thirty-nine other kids that ranged in age from seven to fourteen, one of their daily after-school activities before dinner. She'd just finished pulling in the ones due for a session to see how they were progressing emotionally and psychologically in their environment and schooling.

She smiled at Oz and touched his flame-red hair that was forever tousled. "I'm fine, kiddo. Just fine."

"Are you sure? You look sad."

He didn't have to tell her that he knew what sad looked like because she knew from his file he'd watched his mother battle back her own demons and depression at every turn of his ten-year existence.

It killed Angela to think that he was now worried about her.

"I was just thinking that it's going to be different around here now that Tina is leaving us," she said, speaking of the nine-year-old whose official adoption had just gone through. She'd be leaving Harbor's in the morning, opening up a spot for another needy child.

Her response to Oscar was not completely the truth. But not a lie, either. The place would be much duller without the girl's tinkling laughter.

What would have been worse was to pretend there was nothing wrong at all. She knew that kids were especially tuned in to their parents' or guardians' emotional state. Some attributed it to their survival instinct, developed from the moment they were born. Others to the uglier aspects of life they were exposed to too early.

At any rate, Oz seemed to accept her explanation. Which was good.

"But she's going to have a new family now. That's a good thing, right?"

"That's very definitely a good thing. I'm very happy for her," she agreed. "But that doesn't mean that I'm not going to miss her. Even if we will see her from time to time." When she came back for counseling with her new family to make sure they were bonding as they should.

Oz nodded, as if he completely understood.

Angela had little doubt that he did. Any change in the

compound upset the day-to-day routine that so many of the kids came to count on. It was important to provide consistency since so much had been lacking in their lives before coming there.

"Miss Mitchell! Miss Mitchell!" Jenny, one of the younger girls, came running up to them, ball in hand.

"Jenny, give the others the ball. You're stopping play," another counselor said to her from across the playground.

The girl frowned, but didn't stop. "Miss Mitchell, that soldier from the other day is at the gate."

Angela's pulse quickened. Brian Justice was there? Surely Jenny was mistaken. Maybe another soldier was happening by. She'd circulated fliers at the armory for returning personnel to pick up and had posted a bulletin on the Internet looking for any interest in the program. Perhaps her efforts had generated some response.

Instead, she looked over to see that it was indeed Brian.

Oscar immediately went running over to him before she could stop him. Angela's heart pitched to her feet.

Her mind raced as she tried to come up with a reason he might have stopped by. Something that would explain his presence to the children even now jumping all over him as one of the housemothers allowed him access, but wouldn't end in disappointment for kids that had already been disappointed enough in their short lives.

Whatever it was, she would wait until he reached her and she could see into his eyes….

"WHY'S MISS MITCHELL mad at you?"

Out of the mouths of babes.

Brian wasn't sure where he'd picked up the saying, but it had never rung more true for him as he sat with Oscar on one of the picnic tables. He used the bench seat while Oz was above him on the table. One of the counselors had called for the boy to sit right, but moments after obeying, he'd moved up again. Brian couldn't help feeling that the kid wanted to feel at least equal to him, if not superior.

"Why do you think she's upset with me?" he asked.

Oz shrugged. "She barely looked at you and her smile…it wasn't really a smile."

No, it wasn't, was it?

After what he'd done a couple of nights ago…well, he wasn't exactly pleased with his behavior, either.

Of course, had he been able to forget about her as he had any of a half dozen other one-night stands, he wouldn't be in the position he was now. He would have moved on and would never have seen her again.

But if Angela Mitchell was anything, it wasn't a one-night stand, no matter how hard he tried to convince himself otherwise.

"Maybe I said something she didn't like," he offered.

Oz nodded. "Yeah. I do that sometimes, too. You should tell her you're sorry. That helps."

Brian grinned. Wise kid.

As it stood, the time clock was ticking on his visit. If he'd any doubt about that, all he need do was remember her reaction.

"Hi," Angela had said as the kids led him her way. "How are you, Captain Justice?"

While the words had sounded innocent enough, Brian caught the thread of wariness wound around them.

He'd told her he wanted to further investigate her original invitation. Something flashed in her eyes. Pain, maybe. Doubt. Fear.

As the kids pulled him away to play kickball with

them, he'd caught something else in her face. Fierce warning.

"Don't hurt them," she'd said quietly.

Now, Brian watched the earnest face of the kid sitting next to him.

He'd never given much thought to marriage and children. He supposed part of the reason was that he'd been so consumed with the immediate details of the present, the future was too far away to even contemplate. Oh, his father had talked of an heir when Brian had shared the news that he was switching career tracks, but beyond that, he couldn't imagine his mother welcoming dirty handprints on her designer pants.

He grimaced. Actually, maybe it was just what she needed.

And what about what he needed?

His gaze was immediately drawn to Angela where she was crouched down in front of the girl named Jenny. She looked at him briefly before looking down and then back at the girl, as if he needed watching but she didn't want him to know she felt that way.

Had he done that? If he had, he hadn't meant to. Since they'd exchanged very few words before moving their conversation to her bedroom the other night, he'd figured she understood that it had been about sex and nothing more.

Oh, yeah? If that was the case, what was he doing there now?

"Do you ever have nightmares?"

Brian blinked, surprised by Oscar's question. He searched the open face of the ten-year-old, wondering how he should answer. Since he'd always subscribed to honesty being the best policy, he cleared his throat and said quietly, "Yes. Yes, I do."

Oz nodded. "Me, too."

Brian squinted at him. His problems had dominated so much of his thoughts that he hadn't taken the time to consider that others might be suffering the same symptoms he was. Oh, he was well versed on post-traumatic stress disorder. He just hadn't though that nonmilitary personnel would also suffer from the affliction.

Brian climbed up so that he could sit next to Oz on the tabletop. "Do you have them often?" he asked.

Oz shrugged. "I used to have them every night. But now…maybe every other night. Miss Mitchell says that they'll go away before I know it, but I'm not so sure."

Brian hadn't been aware that's what he was going to do, but he found himself slightly leaning against the kid. And Oz leaned against him. For all intents and purposes, to outside eyes they weren't touching. But Brian knew they were. And he felt such an incredible rush of affection it nearly overwhelmed him.

"Miss Mitchell is pretty smart," Brian said. It seemed impossible that the nightmares he had would one day go away, too. But just like a physical injury, it made sense that psychological wounds would also heal.

Oz added, "She's nice, too. And hot."

Brian chuckled at the adult description as Angela rose to her feet and shielded her eyes against the sinking sun as she took in the playground and the kids dotting it. Then she was looking in their direction.

"I couldn't agree with you more, Oz," he said quietly. "I couldn't agree with you more."

And he leaned a little more into the kid who seemed to be giving him something he hadn't known he needed. And, he hoped, he was giving the same in return.

ANGELA FELT A MIXTURE of fondness and fear as she watched Brian and Oz on the picnic table. The boy might be older than his years, but he was just ten and sometimes he could be so impressionable. He'd been hurt so much in his short life. She couldn't bear it if she were responsible for even more pain. Allowing him to hope for a connection to a man who was incapable of a relationship was like watching a speeding train approach a stretch of broken track.

Marsha, the center's director, stepped up next to her, following her gaze. "So it's happening."

Angela squinted at her. "Pardon me?"

"Your program." She motioned toward the picnic table. "You're pushing ahead with it."

Angela looked down and away, afraid of what Marsha might see. "Yes."

"I see." Marsha's sigh filled the air. "You probably think I'm a cold fish, Angie, but you couldn't be farther off the mark. Where you are now? Every one of us has been. It's not until you get hurt to the point where you believe you'll never heal that you'll learn that if you invest yourself too personally, you're not helping the kids." Her voice dropped. "Or that man over there."

Angela swiveled to look at her.

"Oh, I know. I knew it would happen the moment you pitched your idea."

The dinner bell rang. The kids put their play equipment away and then lined up to go into the main hall where they'd wash their hands and then fill trays with food from the preparation counter.

"Just promise me you'll be careful," Marsha said.

And with that, the director disappeared back into her office where she would likely gather her things and leave for the day. Which is what she should be doing herself.

"Good night, Miss Mitchell! See you tomorrow!" The kids greeted her as they passed.

She smiled and waved.

After the last of them disappeared into the hall, she looked over to where Brian still sat at the picnic table alone. He got up and walked in her direction.

God, but he was more handsome than any man had a right to be. He was in perfect physical shape, yes, but it was more than that. Something in the way he held himself. A pride. A sense of surety, a hint of cockiness, that made her toes curl in her sandals.

But it was the darkness in him that drew her like a moth to a flame.

"Do you eat dinner with them?" he asked.

She shook her head and looked in the direction of the hall. Anywhere but into his eyes, eyes that held that same intense look as the other night. She knew how easily she could fall into their hazel depths. Respond to the need that reached out to her.

"How about having dinner with me, then?" he asked.

She quietly said, "We're not going to my apartment."

"Fair enough. What say we drive to the beach to catch the last of the sunset and then find someplace nearby?"

She didn't say anything for a long time, merely stared at him. Then, "Why?"

He'd assumed a military at ease stance when he'd stopped in front of her, arms behind him, his shoulders back. Now he shifted on his feet. "Because I have an apology to make and it's going to take me that long to figure out how to word it in a way that will guarantee forgiveness."

5

UPON ANGELA'S INSISTENCE, they combined his suggestion: they picked up hot dogs and ate them while walking on the beach. Despite the warm weather, the stretch of white sand was almost deserted; only one other older couple out for a walk with a dog and a couple of men with fold-up chairs fishing. Angela had taken off her sandals and walked closer to the surf, seemingly not caring that every now and again an ambitious wave dampened the bottom of her pants.

"So…talk," she said quietly.

Direct and to the point. He liked that.

He grinned. "Is that any way to talk to a guy who just bought you dinner?"

"After the other night, I figure I'm entitled."

They walked for a little while before she said, "Look, Brian, I know how I must appear in hindsight. I mean, we barely spoke before…well, we slept together." She chewed on her bottom lip and looked out over the darkening Atlantic to her left. "You probably won't believe this, but what happened…it's not something I've ever done before. I'm still surprised by my behavior." She looked at him as if judging his reaction. "But…" She trailed off and looked down at her feet.

"But no matter what, you didn't deserve the way I treated you," he finished for her.

She didn't say anything.

He nodded. "I know. And I'm sorry for that."

He felt her attention on his profile and wondered what was going on in that pretty head of hers. He found out.

"Was it the nightmare?" she asked.

He stiffened, having expected her to go down a more traveled road. Inquire if he had a "girl in every port" or if one-night stands were a regular part of his dating life.

Instead she went straight to the heart of the matter.

He should have been surprised. But he wasn't. Her uncanny ability to see him was the reason why he'd sought out her company.

"Partly," he answered as honestly as possible.

A pair of gulls circled above them and then one dove into the surf.

"I'm not going to lie to you, Angela. The other night I went to your place looking for a one-night stand." He saw her wince. "No, it's not anything you said. Anything you did. You don't have an invisible sign posted on you that says, 'hey, booty calls welcome.'"

This got a thin smile from her.

"It's just that…" What did he say? "It's just that right now I'm in the middle of…"

Was he really on the verge of telling her what was happening in his life? Not even his JAG attorney knew everything. And certainly he hadn't told his friends or family.

He looked into her open, waiting face, and he realized he wanted to tell someone. Not just any someone, he wanted to tell her.

But in light of what had already happened between them, if he revealed the truth about the court-martial, about what had gone down in Iraq, how might she look at him then?

"I'm in the middle of some pretty nasty Corps business right now. And, the fact is, I don't know what the outcome is going to be, or how it's going to impact my life." He cleared his throat and steered her a little farther inland when a large wave crashed ashore. "Now is not the time to start dating anyone."

She seemed to accept his explanation. "This nasty business…it's the cause of your nightmares?"

He gave her a half-smile. "Trust me, you don't want to open that baggage."

She met his gaze fully. "I'm a certified baggage handler, remember?"

The last of the setting sun shone in his eyes. He turned around, facing her as he walked backward, slowing their pace, but blocking the rays from blinding her. "I'm not one of your kids, Angela. You can't fix me."

She glanced away. "Yes, well, I don't seem to do very well fixing them, either."

He stared at her. "Are you kidding me? I'll be the first to admit I'm no expert, but from what I can see you're doing a wonderful job with them."

She didn't seem to be buying it. "You've known me for what? A whole of five minutes?"

He stopped completely and reached out to touch the side of her face. She looked up into his eyes, clearly surprised. "But in those five minutes I've come to know a lot."

A lot that he liked.

She plainly had an impact at Harbor's. The kids adored her as much as she did them. And after what he'd done the other night, any other woman would have told him where to get off and refused him entrance today.

Instead, she had not only let him in, she was giving him a second chance that he hadn't earned or deserved.

And he wanted her with an intensity that fascinated him.

She looked down, forcing him to retract his hand. "God, I don't even know if you're a lifer."

She was referring to his military commitment. "I'm career, yes."

She searched his face. "Married before?"

"No."

"Close?"

"Depends on your definition of close." She waited. "I thought I was. But when I announced I was going to quit the life I'd been bred for and enter the Corps, she dumped me faster than I could drop and do ten."

"Then you weren't close."

"No, I wasn't close."

She squinted into the last rays of the golden sun. "Kids?"

He shook his head. "No. I'm one of the rare specimens who still thinks that a man should learn how to take care of himself, then a wife, before he even considers becoming a father."

"But you want kids."

It was a statement rather than a question. Because of what she'd witnessed between him and Oscar earlier?

"I'd never really thought about it before. Until…"

Until her and her kids.

"And you're returning to duty…when?"

It was his turn to look away.

The sun had slid the rest of the way over the horizon so he turned back around and resumed walking. She hesitated and then followed beside him.

"That's the nasty business you were talking about? Whether or not you return?"

"Something like that."

He wasn't quite ready to tell her he was facing possible court martial. Not yet. But he hoped he could. If she agreed to forgive him his earlier behavior and would continue to see him.

"Don't tell me you're one of those girls who only wants to get involved with officers in the military," he said, only half joking.

Angela's step slowed. "To the contrary. I may romanticize a lot of things, but military service isn't one of them. You may be surprised to know that I'm staunchly antiwar."

He stared at her.

"I'm a pacifist, through and through. 'Give peace a chance,' and 'War, hunh, what is it good for,' group marches on Washington, letters to my congressman and senators, the whole nine."

"Then why did you come to the armory?"

She hesitated slightly. "Because the kids need a few good men in their lives." She looked at him and her voice softened. "And I think one man in particular could use a few good kids in his life."

He didn't say anything.

She cleared her throat. "I'm antiwar, not antimilitary. What compels you and the others is honor and a need to protect God and country... It's your leadership I question. Putting any life at risk should be a last-resort measure." A shadow fell across her face that had nothing to do with clouds in the sky, but rather, he suspected, clouds from within. "I'm not completely ignorant when it comes to the military."

He didn't say anything, waiting for her to explain.

"My mother was an Air Force pilot. She died in Desert Storm."

Brian wondered at the ability she had to continually surprise him.

"I, um, was thirteen and my aunt—my mother's sister—already had six kids of her own and couldn't take me in, no matter the monthly social security checks. And since I never knew who my father was—I'd long guessed that since my mother was career, it was probably someone she served with, maybe married—well, I was given up to the state."

"Angela…" Brian stopped walking.

She took his arm, encouraging him to continue walking. "I didn't have it so bad. I ended up staying in the same foster home until I graduated from high school and earned a scholarship to Florida State, so I had a pretty normal upbringing, I guess. While there wasn't love or affection, my foster sisters and brothers and I were safe, we always had enough to eat, and most of us went on to college. My experience is nothing near what the kids at Harbor's have gone and continue to go through."

Brian tried to imagine life through her eyes. More, what had made her come through it all so balanced and practical and yet idealistic.

They walked quietly for a while. He slid his hand into hers, knowing relief and gratitude when she not only accepted his touch, but returned it.

ANGELA FELT SO THOROUGHLY alive and connected. It was fascinating to think that a couple of hours ago she'd thought she'd never see Captain Brian Justice again.

She tightened her grip on his large, warm hand, wanting him with an intensity that might have frightened her had she not come to the conclusion she had: namely that despite Marsha's warning and her own misgivings, she couldn't be anyone other than who she was.

She was drawn to this man. No matter his sins. No matter what anyone said or did. And to only give herself partially wasn't what she was made of.

And if heartache lay down the path? She refused to think about it. Right now all that mattered was this moment. Him. Her.

"It's getting dark. Maybe we should start heading back," she said quietly, wanting to be alone with him in a place more private than a public beach.

"A little ways more," he said.

After a while, his steps slowed and then drew to a stop altogether. It was almost completely dark, the Atlantic a navy blue roar to her left, the sky a bruised pink to her right. Lights from nearby condos were now brighter than the sky, and the sand beneath her feet seemed to instantly grow cooler without the sun to warm it.

"We're here," Brian said quietly, facing a deck connected to a one-story house just off the beach.

"We're where?"

He looked at her in the growing darkness. "My place."

Angela returned her attention to the house. It was nowhere near as opulent as the nearby multistoried condos, but its location and understated design spoke of someone well-off.

"Rental?"

"Own."

She smiled, hyperaware of the way his thumb caressed her hand. "I'm not going to sleep with you tonight, Brian."

He tucked his chin into his broad chest and chuckled, drawing her close to his side, his arm around her. "At least you didn't say you were never going to sleep with me again." He rubbed her arm. "I have a bike. I can give you a ride back to your car."

"Bike? As in Schwinn?"

"As in Harley."

"Ah."

She cuddled closer to him, turning so that they were face-to-face. The air had grown considerably cooler and his warmth was so tantalizing. "There's no hurry."

He bent down, hesitating slightly before kissing her.

Angela sighed into him, loving the salty taste of his mouth.

Minutes ticked by and she knew that he was bent on proving her a liar. More of making out with him and she was going to go back on her pledge not to sleep with him tonight. Her entire body felt like a live wire and he was the only man capable of handling her.

She forced her mouth from his and gasped for breath against his chest.

He threaded his fingers through her hair.

"I can't promise you anything beyond the moment, Angela. Not right now."

She pressed her nose against him. "That nasty Corps business," she whispered.

"Yes."

She nodded. "Just so I know that going in…well, I can't promise everything will be okay. But right now I want you so much that I can't think about what lies around the next bend."

He groaned and kissed her again, hard, probing. Then he led her to the deck stairs by the hand, a man not about to refuse a needy woman….

6

Two weeks later...

TODAY BRIAN HAD NEVER FELT more like Captain Justice in his eight-year career. He was in full marine dress blues, Mameluke sword and white hat. He had the latter tucked under his left arm now as he stood out in the hall with Tom Kushman, his JAG attorney, who just explained how everything would proceed, when he was to stand and sit, and warned him against interrupting the proceedings.

Not that Brian intended to. He was facing what was coming to him. He had been the supervising officer on that assignment so responsibility fell completely on him. No one else. His men were blameless. Including Chris Conrad, who should never have been on the mission.

Of course, none of that would come into play today. This was a hearing to determine if there was enough evidence to hold him over for trial. Which was already a forgone conclusion in his book since a crime had been committed, innocent civilians had died, and someone had to pay the price. That someone was him.

The courtroom door opened and a military bailiff told them the judge was ready.

Brian followed his attorney in and they took their seats to the left of the courtroom. He looked over at the prosecutor's table, not recognizing any of the three military attorneys there. They were in conference, speaking in hushed tones, never once sparing him a glance.

He scanned the gallery, finding what looked like a reporter scribbling something on her notepad, and a couple of other uniformed personnel, perhaps there to observe the proceedings for their own purposes.

It was the sight of Chris Conrad that caught him off guard.

Like him, he was in full uniform, his back ramrod straight…as was his gaze.

That day crashed into Brian like a twenty-foot brick wall, the impact robbing him of his cool reserve. He leaned toward his attorney. "What's Lance Corporal Conrad doing here?"

Before he could get a response, the bailiff called the court to attention. Everyone rose and the judge entered and took the bench.

The bailiff read the charges and the judge indicated that the prosecution should proceed in proving they had the evidence to convict.

When the prosecutor called Conrad to offer testimony, Brian leaned into his attorney again. "What in the hell is he doing here?"

He soon found out. Conrad was there to help nail his ass to the wall.

Brian had expected to be punished. As the highest-ranking officer and team leader, it had been his responsibility to see that assignments were carried through without incident. But to have one of his own men testifying against him was something else entirely.

"So it's your testimony, Lance Corporal Conrad, that Captain Brian Justice, the defendant, was responsible for the civilian casualties."

He leaned forward to speak into the mike, not blinking when he said, "Yes, sir. It is."

The courtroom door opened. Brian was so focused on Conrad's face that he didn't immediately look at who had entered. But whoever it was caused the marine to go pale and sit back in his chair as if knocked there by a sucker punch.

Brian slowly turned his head to see the other members of his team: Eric Armstrong, Eddie Cash and Mateo Guerrero in full uniform. They sat, one by one, in the back row.

"What's going on?" he asked his attorney.

Kushman smiled. "Reinforcements."

The prosecutor finished his questioning and Kushman stood up. "Lance Corporal…in light of recent developments, would you like to amend your statement to the court?"

OUTSIDE THE COURTROOM a half hour later, Brian shook Eric's, Eddie's and then Matt's hands, giving them each a hearty bear hug.

"What in the hell are you all doing here?"

Matt puffed out his chest. "You didn't really think we were going to let you go down for this, did you?"

Eddie added, "Conrad is nothing but a lying, steaming sack of mule shit. If he'd have just let things lay, charges would never have been brought against you and he would have avoided prosecution himself. Instead he tried to cover his own ass by testifying against you."

Now Conrad was the one facing charges of manslaughter and Brian's case had been dismissed without prejudice.

Definitely not how he'd seen everything going down.

"Thanks, man," Brian said. "You all saved my six, big-time."

"You'd have done the same for any one of us," Eric said.

Yes, he would have. Although he hadn't asked them for anything, they'd stood up for him. Traveled to Richmond. Given him his life back.

"You know, I still should be facing punishment for this," he said somberly. "Two civilians died that day. If I had been doing my job, they'd still be alive."

"Come on, Cap, we all know that Conrad was an IED looking for a place to go off. It just happened to go down on your watch," Matt said. "If you're guilty, then so are we."

And that was the gist of it, wasn't it? They'd all carry around that day for the rest of their lives, no matter if charges were brought or dropped.

"So," Eddie said, slapping him on the back. "I'd say today earned us at least dinner and a round of drinks."

Brian threw back his head and laughed, grateful for these men who were not only fellow marines, but also friends. He'd be serving again with Matt and Eric, while Eddie was enjoying life after active duty…at least for now. But he knew that their connection was forever. Being a marine wasn't something you did, it was who you were.

Epilogue

WAS IT REALLY ONLY FOUR WEEKS ago that he'd come stateside, completely expecting his life to come crashing down around his ears? Brian wondered. Since he was heading back overseas for his next assignment in Afghanistan, he guessed it was. And, oh, how his life had changed. In large ways and small. And none quite the way he'd expected.

"I can't believe you're leaving already," Angela had said to him the night before. "It feels like you just got here."

He felt the same. Not physically. In that regard, it seemed he'd been home a lifetime given all that had transpired. But on a level he was ill-equipped to define, he realized he had just arrived.

He'd reluctantly released Angela and she'd said goodbye to him, clinging to him as if she might not ever let go.

But ultimately she'd had to.

And he'd had to let go of her.

That morning he'd woken up alone and taken a cab to Miami International Airport to catch a civilian plane back to Richmond, Virginia. It was during the ride that he realized that when all was said and done, he wasn't all that unlike Angela's children at Harbor's: childhood to them was something to survive. And for guys like him, military men, the risk of death was easy; it was the fear of living that scared the pants off them.

"I'll write you an e-mail every day," Oscar had told him when he'd visited Harbor's the last time.

Brian had gripped his shoulder. "Why don't we shoot for once a week, kiddo?"

Odd that before he had lived to ship out and now he couldn't wait to get back.

"Justice!"

Brian turned to find Mateo Guerrero advancing on him in full fatigues as the troops lined up to board the plane that would take them first to Germany and then back to Iraq. He gave his fellow marine a man hug and then stood back to look him over.

"I guess I don't have to ask what you did during your leave," he said with a grin.

"Even if you did, I wouldn't tell you."

They chuckled and turned to watch a young couple kissing off to the side of the airstrip. A gathering of family members had come to see the troops off. The sight used to fill Brian with a sense of isolation. Not anymore. He had little doubt that Angela and the kids would be waiting for him to return, with Oz's freckled face leading the pack.

"Holy shit."

"What is it, Guerrero?" he asked.

"There's my wife and kids."

Brian squinted in the direction Matt was looking, immediately spotting an ageless Latina with long black hair shielding her eyes from the sun. She was flanked by two older kids, one boy and one girl, and had another younger girl in front of her.

He looked back at Guerrero, who seemed rooted to the spot.

He knew they were from Ohio, and suspected that Matt hadn't anticipated seeing his family here in Virginia.

He watched as the usually cool marine dropped his duffel and charged toward his family, pulling his wife over the barricade and hugging her as if they were teenagers rather than older adults.

Brian grinned, knowing that these few minutes would be enough to see Matt through whatever war brought his way....

As for the other guys, it looked like their new missions had been successfully accomplished.

* * * * *

*Celebrate 60 years of pure reading pleasure with
Harlequin® Books!*

*Harlequin Romance® is celebrating by showering
you with DIAMOND BRIDES in February 2009.
Six stories that promise to bring a touch of sparkle to
your life, with diamond proposals and dazzling
weddings, sparkling brides and gorgeous grooms!*

*Enjoy a sneak peek at Caroline Anderson's
TWO LITTLE MIRACLES,
available February 2009 from Harlequin Romance®.*

'I'VE FOUND HER.'

Max froze.

It was what he'd been waiting for since June, but now—now he was almost afraid to voice the question. His heart stalling, he leaned slowly back in his chair and scoured the investigator's face for clues. 'Where?' he asked, and his voice sounded rough and unused, like a rusty hinge.

'In Suffolk. She's living in a cottage.'

Living. His heart crashed back to life, and he sucked in a long, slow breath. All these months he'd feared—

'Is she well?'

'Yes, she's well.'

He had to force himself to ask the next question. 'Alone?'

The man paused. 'No. The cottage belongs to a man called John Blake. He's working away at the moment, but he comes and goes.'

God. He felt sick. So sick he hardly registered the next few words, but then gradually they sank in. 'She's got *what?*'

'Babies. Twin girls. They're eight months old.'

'Eight—?' he echoed under his breath. 'They must be his.'

He was thinking out loud, but the P.I. heard and corrected him.

'Apparently not. I gather they're hers. She's been there since mid-January last year, and they were born during the summer—June, the woman in the post office thought. She was more than helpful. I think there's been a certain amount of speculation about their relationship.'

He'd just bet there had. God, he was going to kill her. Or Blake. Maybe both of them.

'Of course, looking at the dates, she was presumably pregnant when she left you, so they could be yours, or she could have been having an affair with this Blake character before…'

He glared at the unfortunate P.I. 'Just stick to your job. I can do the math,' he snapped, swallowing the unpalatable possibility that she'd been unfaithful to him before she'd left. 'Where is she? I want the address.'

'It's all in here,' the man said, sliding a large envelope across the desk to him. 'With my invoice.'

'I'll get it seen to. Thank you.'

'If there's anything else you need, Mr Gallagher, any further information—'

'I'll be in touch.'

'The woman in the post office told me Blake was away at the moment, if that helps,' he added quietly, and opened the door.

Max stared down at the envelope, hardly daring to open it, but when the door clicked softly shut behind the P.I., he eased up the flap, tipped it and felt his breath jam in his throat as the photos spilled out over the desk.

Oh, lord, she looked gorgeous. Different, though. It took him a moment to recognise her, because she'd grown her hair, and it was tied back in a ponytail, making her look younger and somehow freer. The blond highlights were gone, and it was back to its natural soft golden-brown, with a little curl in the end of the ponytail that he wanted to thread his finger through and tug, just gently, to draw her back to him.

Crazy. She'd put on a little weight, but it suited her. She looked well and happy and beautiful, but oddly, considering how desperate he'd been for news of her for the past year—one year, three weeks and two days, to be exact—it wasn't only Julia who held his attention after the initial shock. It was the babies sitting side by side in a supermarket trolley. Two identical and absolutely beautiful little girls.

* * * * *

When Max Gallagher hires a P.I. to find his estranged wife, Julia, he discovers she's not alone—she has twin baby girls, and they might be his. Now workaholic Max has just two weeks to prove that he can be a wonderful husband and father to the family he wants to treasure.

Look for TWO LITTLE MIRACLES
by Caroline Anderson,
available February 2009 from Harlequin Romance®.

CELEBRATE
60 YEARS
OF PURE READING PLEASURE
WITH HARLEQUIN®!

We'll be spotlighting a different series
every month throughout 2009
to celebrate our 60th anniversary.

Look for Harlequin® Romance in February!

**Harlequin® Romance is celebrating by showering
you with Diamond Brides in February 2009.**

Six stories that promise to bring a touch of sparkle to
your life, with diamond proposals and dazzling weddings,
sparkling brides and gorgeous grooms!

Collect all six books in February 2009,
featuring *Two Little Miracles* by Caroline Anderson.

*Look for the Diamond Brides miniseries
in February 2009!*

www.eHarlequin.com   HRBRIDES09

HARLEQUIN® Romance®

This February the Harlequin® Romance series
will feature six Diamond Brides stories featuring
diamond proposals and gorgeous grooms.

Share your dream wedding proposal and you could WIN!

The most romantic entry will win a diamond
necklace and will inspire a proposal in one of
our upcoming Diamond Grooms books in 2010.

In 100 words or less, tell us the most romantic
way that you dream of being proposed to.

For more information, and to enter
the Diamond Brides Proposal contest, please visit
www.DiamondBridesProposal.com

Or mail your entry to us at:
IN THE U.S.: 3010 Walden Ave., P.O. Box 9069, Buffalo, NY 14269-9069
IN CANADA: 225 Duncan Mill Road, Don Mills, ON M3B 3K9

You're invited to join our Tell Harlequin Reader Panel!

By joining our new reader panel you will:

- Receive Harlequin® books—they are FREE and yours to keep with no obligation to purchase anything!
- Participate in fun online surveys
- Exchange opinions and ideas with women just like you
- Have a say in our new book ideas and help us publish the best in women's fiction

In addition, you will have a chance to win great prizes and receive special gifts! See Web site for details. Some conditions apply. Space is limited.

To join, visit us at
www.TellHarlequin.com.

REQUEST YOUR FREE BOOKS!

2 FREE NOVELS PLUS 2 FREE GIFTS!

HARLEQUIN®

Blaze™

Red-hot reads!

YES! Please send me 2 FREE Harlequin® Blaze™ novels and my 2 FREE gifts (gifts are worth about $10). After receiving them, if I don't wish to receive any more books, I can return the shipping statement marked "cancel". If I don't cancel, I will receive 6 brand-new novels every month and be billed just $4.24 per book in the U.S. or $4.71 per book in Canada, plus 25¢ shipping and handling per book and applicable taxes, if any*. That's a savings of 15% or more off the cover price! I understand that accepting the 2 free books and gifts places me under no obligation to buy anything. I can always return a shipment and cancel at any time. Even if I never buy another book, the two free books and gifts are mine to keep forever.

151 HDN ERVA 351 HDN ERUX

Name	(PLEASE PRINT)	
Address		Apt. #
City	State/Prov.	Zip/Postal Code

Signature (if under 18, a parent or guardian must sign)

Mail to the **Harlequin Reader Service:**
IN U.S.A.: P.O. Box 1867, Buffalo, NY 14240-1867
IN CANADA: P.O. Box 609, Fort Erie, Ontario L2A 5X3

Not valid to current subscribers of Harlequin Blaze books.

Want to try two free books from another line?
Call 1-800-873-8635 or visit www.morefreebooks.com.

* Terms and prices subject to change without notice. N.Y. residents add applicable sales tax. Canadian residents will be charged applicable provincial taxes and GST. Offer not valid in Quebec. This offer is limited to one order per household. All orders subject to approval. Credit or debit balances in a customer's account(s) may be offset by any other outstanding balance owed by or to the customer. Please allow 4 to 6 weeks for delivery. Offer available while quantities last.

Your Privacy: Harlequin Books is committed to protecting your privacy. Our Privacy Policy is available online at www.eHarlequin.com or upon request from the Reader Service. From time to time we make our lists of customers available to reputable third parties who may have a product or service of interest to you. If you would prefer we not share your name and address, please check here. ☐

HB0

COMING NEXT MONTH

#447 BLAZING BEDTIME STORIES Kimberly Raye, Leslie Kelly, Rhonda Nelson
Who said fairy tales are just for kids? Three intrepid Blaze heroines decide to take a break from reality—and discover, to their personal satisfaction, just how sexy happily-ever-afters can be....

#448 SOMETHING WICKED Julie Leto
Josie Vargas has always believed in love at first sight—and once she meets lawman Rick Fernandez, she's a goner. If only he didn't have those demons stalking him....

#449 THE CONCUBINE Jade Lee
Blaze Historicals
Chen Ji Yue has the chance to bring the ultimate honor to her family if she is chosen as one of the new emperor's wives. Of course, first she has to beat out the other three hundred virgins vying for the position. And then she has to stay out of the bed of Sun Bo Tao, the emperor's best friend.

#450 SHE THINKS HER EX IS SEXY... Joanne Rock
24 Hours: Lost
After a very public quarrel with her boyfriend, rock star Romeo Jinks, actress Shannon Leigh just wants to get her life back. But when she finds herself stranded in the Sonoran Desert with her ex, she learns that great sex can make breaking up hard to do.

#451 ABLE-BODIED Karen Foley
Uniformly Hot!
Delta Force operator Ransom Bennett is used to handling anything that comes his way. But debilitating headaches have put him almost out of action. Luckily, his new neighbor, Hannah Hartwell, knows how to handle his pain...and him, too.

#452 UNDER THE INFLUENCE Nancy Warren
Forbidden Fantasies
Sexy bartender Johnny Santini mixes one wicked martini. Or so business exec Natalie Fanshaw discovers, sitting at his bar one lonely Valentine's night. Could a fling with him be a recipe for disaster? Well, she could always claim to be under the influence....

HBCNMBPA0109R2